ALIAS DRAGONFLY
JANE SINGER

YOUNG ADULT HISTORICAL * CIVIL WAR, WASHINGTON, D.C.
AUTHOR RESIDENCE: SOUTHERN CALIFORNIA

Publishing November 15, 2011 in trade paperback 14.95
and ebook 12.95
AVAILABLE VIA INGRAM, BRODART, BAKER & TAYLOR

Optioned for feature film by Halcyon
ISBN THIS REVIEW COPY ONLY: 978-1466316799
COPYRIGHT 2011 JANE SINGER

"Don't love a spy," warns fifteen year old Pinkerton agent **Maddie Bradford**, a lonely, rebellious outsider with a mind on fire and a photographic memory. It is 1861, the Civil War has just started and this motherless teen must move with her soldier-father from New Hampshire to Washington, DC; a city at war, packed cheek by jowl with soldiers, Rebel spies, slave catchers, and traitors of all stripes bent on waging a war of destruction against the Union, and President Lincoln himself.

Maddie's journal, written in secret, of course, begins with her arrival at her aunt's DC boardinghouse through the first year of the Civil War, a time as Maddie puts it, "full of dips and dangers," when she becomes a fearless Union spy. And then there is the mysterious, maddening Jake Whitestone, a young man who awakens something equally dangerous in Maddie: Love in a time of terror.

Civil War historian, author, and lecturer Jane Singer brings her unique voice to Alias Dragonfly.

BELL BRIDGE BOOKS * MEMPHIS, TN * WWW.BELLBRIDGEBOOKS.COM
Contact Deborah Smith, Editor, deborahsmith@bellebooks.com

DEDICATION PAGE

For my brother James Martin Singer

Prologue


The nightmare came again, spreading like an ink stain over my brain …

*I am alone in the alley. Stealthy as a cellar rat, the girl creeps up behind me. I'm too busy fishing her dispatch out of a slops bucket to sense her. It is too late to pull my revolver from my boot. I feel hers in my back.*

*"Turn around, Yankee." She whispers. I face her full on. I gasp. We are so alike: wide-set blue eyes –starburst eyes flecked with green, rambling brown curls, and tall, close in age—young, we are young. We are wearing wrinkled black frocks that hang loose on our thin frames. Are we in mourning, or in disguise? We might pass for sisters. But I don't have a sister, not a living one.*

*She cocks her revolver . . .*

*I duck low, and dart past her down the long, narrow alleyway. A bullet whizzes past my cheek and smashes into the wall as I run toward the street.*

*She does not take her kill shot.*

*She wants to capture me if she can, parade me before her handlers—her prize. I hear her panting behind me like a slave-tracking hound after its quarry. She catches me by the ankle. I fly forward and hit the ground. She is leaning over me, trying to pull me up. I rake my fingers down her face. She bleeds.*

*Kick, like they taught you, fight, I tell myself. I slam the heel of my boot into her kneecap.*

*Before she buckles, she punches me in the mouth. I am bleeding, too. She is down. Her weapon clatters to the cobblestones. In that instant, I pull my pistol out of my boot.*

*Behind me, I hear a man, his voice slurred by drink, ask, "Anything broke, sweetheart?"*

*I hear her snarling, like a wild thing.*

*"Little witch. Bit me, did you?" He yelps.*

*I can hear him cursing as he totters away. She is clutching her leg, crawling toward her weapon. I grab it up, and yank her to her feet. I jam my gun into her side.*

*"Walk," I tell her. She sways, her teeth clenched, in pain.*

*"Yankee devil." She hisses.*

*I am near my boss's headquarters. Even in the darkness, with the moon smudged by clouds, I see it. I pull her along, past two Union soldiers who eye us, leering.*

*"Don't ever let me catch you out drinking again, Nancy." I say loudly, holding her against me, supporting her. "If papa saw you like this, he'd beat you blue."*

*The soldiers laugh as I drag her along.*

*Three men guarding Mr. Pinkerton's door, step aside at the sight of me.*

*Inside, the girl collapses in a chair, her head down. I tie her hands together, avoiding the blazing hatred in her eyes.*

*Mr. P. hands me his handkerchief. I wipe at my bloody lip.*

*He walks to the girl. "This time, lassie, we win."*

*She throws back her head. She is laughing.*

*The room explodes in a flash of blinding white light. I am no longer flesh. I am in pieces—bone, bits of skin and glass.*

I am screaming. I cover my mouth to muffle the sound, and fumble for the revolver I keep by my pillow: The smooth wooden stock, the cold metal barrel warms in my hand.

Breathe. Slow, easy. Breathe.

Something tugs me toward wakefulness. It is the easy light of dawn, soft and gray, slowing the thudding of my heart.

I am angry at this nightmare, like it is a living being. Much of it, not all, but much of it is wrong.

Write it down, then, the truth, the way it really happened, how it all began, I tell myself. Take up pen and paper. Write.


One

You've probably guessed by now that I am a spy.

We are slippery sorts, like the eels that slither out of my father's fishnets back in Portsmouth, New Hampshire. That's where I was born and lived until we came to Washington City.

You might pass me on the street and not even know it. I could be the one-armed beggar with a half-moon scar on her forehead, the orphan under the gas lamp selling wilted violets, or the young woman in crimson velvet awaiting her escort to one of President Lincoln's White House balls.

Or maybe I am the lanky serving maid with a mass of springy, light brown curls. I might be the muleskinner's brat, with blue eyes in a dirty face, my hands stained from tanning animal hides.

Sometimes I am known as "Fiona," or "Dragonfly." These are aliases, fake names given to me by Mr. Alan Pinkerton, so my true identity and movements can remain secret.

Between missions, I stay in Washington City, in my aunt's boarding house that is my sometime stopping place, not really my home.

My father is a private with the 2$^{nd}$ New Hampshire Infantry regiment. Brave men like him aim to win the fight against the Confederates. If that happens, the Negro slaves might well go free. I'd never seen human beings dragged like cattle to auction until I came to Washington City. Their freedom, and putting our broken country back together, my father says, is worth dying for. I agree with my whole heart. Even about the dying part.

Some call this conflict between the North and the South the Civil War. That's a bunch of bosh! There is nothing civil about it. After more than a year it still rages, destroying everything in its path.

And here I am smack in the middle of it, a girl of fifteen who never believed she'd fit in anywhere, let alone contribute to a great cause. In spite of the danger, I am bursting proud to do my part. Bursting proud and changed forever.

Here then, is the story of the lonely kid I was; roaming in the forest at all hours of the night—and after an accident, how I became a homebound misfit with a fired-up brain that rattled and sped like a runaway engine, and why I am, I think, becoming a woman.

I write in secret, of course.

*

No chapter break
Make this (above) the first scene of chapter one


May 1861
Portsmouth, New Hampshire


The day Papa and I went to Washington City, I felt like a cook pot that was about to boil over: A bone-cracking heat was rising in me. Angry, I was. Scared.

"You've enlisted for three years, Papa? No!"

He was all I had and I loved him mightily.

9

"I thought it was only going to be for three months?" *And how dare you wait until the day we leave to tell me. Did you think I'd run away again? Well I just might.*

"Mr. Lincoln has called us up for much longer, Maddie. I'm in until we win this war," he said, closing the door of the snug little cabin he'd crafted with his own hands for mama and me. It was perched high and isolated, up a rutted, rock-strewn path that ended on the banks of the twisty, whirling Piscataqua River.

My father's clear-cut thin face, even thinner since Mama died, looked really scary-gaunt. He tried to stroke my hair but his fingers caught in my mess of pop-out frizzy curls as I turned away. I didn't labor to brush my hair that often. I didn't give a tinker's damn how I looked. Especially since Mama had died six months and three days before. I was dressed in a black bombazine, mourning gown that was left in a paper wrapper at our door by two townswomen who scurried away when I appeared at the window. The 'village peculiar,' I was to them. Odd as a five - legged goose.

A ruffle of cold wind sweeping up from the river made me shiver. I put on my traveling cape with the tattered blue silk lining. I pulled the oversized hood over my head, just to my eyes, making me look like a gypsy-spirit.

As I turned away from the cabin, a shimmer of sunlight on the front window made me think I saw a bright-cheeked glowing face, a tumble of red hair, and the greenest of green eyes; the way mama was before the wasting sickness took her. But when a feathery cloud drifted over the sun, she was gone. Gone to shadow.

*Goodbye Mama.*

Papa hefted our travel trunk on his back and handed me his haversack. "Don't look back," he said, rubbing his eyes.

I ran ahead of him down the rocky walk to the end of the road to wait for the wagons that would carry my father's regiment to the train depot: The grocers, doctors, fishermen like my dad, the plowmen, and their sons - not much older than I was.

*I'm just as strong as any of them. Why in Hades do I have to stay in Washington City with an aunt I've never met?*

"I'm keeping with you, Papa. I'll fight too."

"You'll do nothing of the kind. It's a man's war, Maddie."

"Bosh! I'm tall as a man already," I said, straightening my sharp-edged, bony knees and jamming a black derby hat down on my head. Fact is, over that year I'd grown so much I figured if I kept going my head would shoot straight through the roof of the cabin and I'd be fit for a zoo.

My father's uniform, a red fox tail jacket and blue trousers looked new and stiff. He looked stiff too. At that moment I truly hated everything about the 2nd

New Hampshire Regiment right down to the buttons on my father's coat that glittered like fool's gold.

"Well, Private Summoner Bradford," I said, with a whole lot of sass, "You think you can shoot some Rebels in your fine, starched uniform? You look like a statue."

My father stood straight as a larch tree and tried to look down at me, even though we were nearly eye-to-eye.

"Madeline Eve Bradford, do not ever speak to me that way again. Mind me, and mind my sister, do you understand?"

*No. I don't understand.*

"I'm all tangled up, Papa." *Like knotted seaweed battered by a thousand ocean waves.* I turned away and picked up a smooth river rock. I held its coolness to my burning cheek.

"Is it the leaving? We'll come back here, someday, I promise."

"No! I don't care if we ever do, and neither do you, Papa, and that is the truth, isn't it?"

"Just to visit their graves, now and again, that's all." He said softly. "Now and again."

"I don't need to look at a patch of rocky ground with headstones jutting up to think of Mama and Nancy."

Hurt, like a shadow crossed my father's face. They'd lost a daughter when she was about three and I was two. Just before my accident I'd found a death record in Mama's trunk with a name on it I didn't recognize.

"Who was Nancy?" I asked. "What did she look like?"

And because I was a little kid and mama looked like she was about to wash away in a flood of tears like they'd been stored in a full-up rain barrel, I figured her upset was my fault.

"Like you," she finally said. She looked just like you. Beautiful, she was."

*Beautiful? I'm plain, like an unpainted fence.*

"Papa? What happened to Nancy?" He bit down on his knuckles and closed his eyes.

"She came out right at first, then when she was around two she stopped crying and her body froze up. Doctors couldn't do anything. When she was three, she died."

*And that's why after the accident you wouldn't let me out of your sight? Or was it always that way?*

"Did she play with me? With anyone?"

"At first."

*Maybe I remembered her. Eyes like starbursts, rosy skin, a freckle or two.*

But she was a big fat secret, this sister of mine. How could they have kept her from me? They wouldn't, I decided. I made up a life for her, as if she'd not died at all. It was though I'd woven her on mama's loom, spun and shaped her into a reckless, free-roaming, saucy girl.

*Nancy, Nancy, tickling Nancy, you'd face down she-wolves in the forest, sashay around the village in a red frock with all the boys following you, asking you to kiss them. Sometimes you would.*

Puffs of imaginings like pollen clusters swirled in my head as Papa and I waited for the wagons.

It seemed like they were taking forever to come. The road was empty. A strong wind from the river, marsh-musky and chilled, rattled through the birches.

"Where in *hadees* are the wagons, Papa?"

"Mind your mouth, Madeline."

"I'll cook for you in camp, clean your rifle, shine your boots, anything!"

"No! That would be too dangerous. You are all I have, do you understand?"

"What if something happens to you? I was shouting. "I won't be there. You need me!"

"Enough. You will stay with my sister, in her boardinghouse. There's an end on it."

My father's mouth was set tight like a freshly caught clam. There was no sense arguing with him anymore.

"Fine. Great. Right." I kicked at a rock until my toe was throbbing, sending flashes of pain straight to my heart.

Finally, out of a spray of pebbles and dust came the wagons pulled by lumbering dray horses; teeming with new soldiers bright as penny whistles, readying for Mr. Lincoln's War. They were waving flags, whistling and cheering. Hands, white gloved, ready hands; eager hands pulled us up onto a flat board seat. I clutched Papa's haversack to my chest, the way I wanted to clutch him, hard, never letting go. The wagon pitched and rolled like it was borne by an ocean wave carrying us away, and nothing could stop it until we washed up, a pile of bleached bones on the shore.

Two

We got to the Portsmouth train depot to ride the iron monster, the train that would take us through Boston and Baltimore to Washington City. There were masses of people spreading like a cloud of mosquitoes along the tracks. I ducked down just as a man hurled a flaming torch over my head. It landed a bull's eye square in the middle of a ragged Confederate flag. The flag caught fire, sending red sparks into a crowd of whooping and yelling soldiers, bawling women and scared little kids clinging to their mama's skirts.

"Dear God," my father said, putting his arm tightly around me. It didn't happen often. It felt good. I leaned against him.

"Don't leave go of me, Maddie."

*I won't, not ever. Not if I can help it.*

"Hooo-ee, kill all those rebels!" Someone screeched. Another torch thudded into a hay bale making the whole thing go up in flames.

"Oh my darling will I ever see you again?" A woman cried, clinging to a soldier.

"Don't you die now, daddy," a tiny girl sobbed. Strands of her hair were caught up in the buttons of her father's coat as he hoisted her in the air.

My head was buzzing and pictures of all I was seeing were clicking past my eyes.

It was my first ever ride on a train—actually, it was my first real trip to anywhere. Once I saw the locomotive engines on rickety tracks, pulling a row of carriages into Portsmouth village, and many times I'd heard train whistles screaming high over the Piscataqua River back in New Hampshire, but I had never boarded one.

My father steered me along. The train car heaved and shuddered as people piled in.

We bumped and wove along through the narrow aisles into high-backed worn, plush seats. As the engine rumbled, spitting ashes and coal smoke through the windows, I started shaking.

"Are you all right, Maddie?"

He really wanted to know if I was having one of the spells I'd had for a few years after I fell out of a tree when I was six years old. The fall smack down on a river rock left me with a mark in the shape of a half-moon on my forehead.

*What were you doing, Maddie, up there so high in the tree?* Maybe *I was trying to fly away, Papa, away from mama's fevered face, her groans at night that froze me in my bed. And the way you stopped smiling, and scolded me for no good reason.*

Bosh! That wasn't it. I didn't tell him the truth and I never will. Fact is, I thought I heard Nancy calling to me that night, taunting me, telling me to crawl out on that tree limb, high above the forest-floor.

After my fall, I healed up okay but the spells I had were the kind that sent me to my knees when far-away sounds were loud as thunder and made a ruckus in my brain. Because they were so worried about me, Mama and Papa never left me alone and I couldn't go to Mrs. Margery Middleton's Day School like the rest of the village kids. So I was taught at home. Homebound. *A barnacle-girl stuck fast to a rock, waves crashing over her with no way to break free.*

Don't get me wrong. I loved learning. We devoured books, savored them like maple-sugared porridge, clustered around our hearth reading to each other night after night. Papa's calloused hands carefully turning the pages of Mr. Shakespeare's sonnets. Mama reciting them by heart, looking moon-eyed at Papa, and cuddling me.

I teared up,, remembering, as the train rattled along.

"I'm okay, I guess."

I kept breathing deeply. The spells had pretty much stopped when I was about eleven. But often I felt my fired-up brain working way too hard. It was like colors, and shapes and images swarmed together. And whether I wanted to or not, by day's end I remembered the smallest details of nearly every hour that had passed. It was overwhelming.

As I got older, I'd learned a few tricks to calm myself down. Instead of crouching low and covering my ears when things were spinning and whirling around me, I'd count . . . everything: The dots on the top of a strawberry, dust motes, fallen leaves, you get the idea. Then I'd file away all I'd seen and heard for whenever I wanted to recall it. And I sure tried like the dickens to act normal.

Just so you see what I mean, here is what I saw on the train. There were three hundred and seventy two brass buttons on the soldiers' jackets as they pushed past us to their seats. Each soldier had a different smile or glower, or even teary eyes. Five had moustaches that twirled up like crescent-moons; six had the kind that curved down the sides of their mouths. Ten had whiskers that crisscrossed their chins.

Sorry, I couldn't help myself. I had to tell you. *Square up, Maddie*, I told myself over the gabble of the train wheels and the shouts of the soldiers. *Your father doesn't need any more to worry about now*.

"I'm truly sorry I got so mad back at the cabin, Papa I'm afraid for you."

Papa touched my cheek—the way he used to touch Mama's, all the love he had for her seemed like it was bursting through his fingers. Then, she'd sweep us both into her arms, her fire-red hair spilling like a warm curtain over our faces.

"I'm afraid too, Maddie, but as sure as I breathe, I know I'm doing the right thing."

As we neared Baltimore, we passed through a tunnel. It was dark as pitch as the train rattled and chuffed along the track. *"Old Abe did creep straight in this way, disguised in Scotch cap, but plain as day,"* a young soldier sang, smelling of spirits and crammed tight against my shoulder. "Hooray for Father Abraham!" yelled another.

"You watch what you say, brother," a voice hissed. "Half the rats on this train might be Rebels in on the plot to get Lincoln, so shut it."

My father turned back to the soldiers behind us. "What do you mean?" Papa asked.

"There was a plot afoot to kill the great man here in Baltimore, led by a barber and his band of weasels," the soldier answered, pulling a tiny flask from his coat and downing the contents fast. He wore wire-rimmed spectacles that made him look like schoolteacher. Maybe he was.

"Back in February, President Abraham Lincoln was due to be set upon as soon as he reached Baltimore," the soldier said. "There were some who didn't want him to make it to Washington City to be inaugurated. It seems a railroad man named Fulton hired Detective Alan Pinkerton, who operated out of Chicago, to come to Washington City to foil the plot. Pinkerton sent his best spy to infiltrate the band of conspirators."

"Did he?" my father asked.

"Yes, he did. Posing as a Confederate, he got their confidence." To be able to do that, to be someone else excited me.

"To be sure, the Pinkerton men and one fine lady snuck our good President into Washington City on this very route," another man said, catching our conversation as he walked by.

"Disguised as a six-foot-tall ailing man in a shawl Old Abe was, for the love of God," a soldier bellowed, laughing.

"That's right," said the passing man. I looked him over. He was not a soldier that I could tell. He was wore a dark wool suit with a purple cravat, and a gold pin studded with pearls. He had a small canvas travel bag and carried a writing pad. I couldn't help but have a quick read of the jottings as he walked quickly past our seats. I made out a few words just by glancing down. This is what I read:

**Rebel General Beauregard threatens Washington Invasion.**
**Dispatch intercepted.**

When he saw me peering down at his pad, he covered it quickly and frowned. He had slicked-back blond hair and a long face.

"Who's this dandy?" a soldier yelled. "Maybe the train has got some Reb spies on it after all."

15

"I'm with the *Washington Intelligencer* newspaper, sir, and a loyal Union man," the man said. "I'm here in plain sight, not disguised like some of those New York reporters that favor the enemy."

"Bully for you!" shouted another soldier. "My old uncle down in Washington City got clapped in the Old Capitol Prison just for calling Lincoln an ape."

"Boo hoo!" someone yelled. "Let him rot, and all the others that's traitors!"

I thought about this. "Do they put people in jail just for speaking out against the president, Papa?"

"Apparently so, Maddie."

"Do women do such things as spying, Papa?" I asked.     "Maybe they do, but that is hardly a woman's work."

*A woman's work ... Sewing, rolling pie dough, having babies, or being a governess, sleeping in a cold garret in a big house. And of course we couldn't be soldiers.*

.     "I'd bed a lady spy, sure," a rattle-voiced soldier said aloud over the gabble and groan of the train.     "Quiet down, brother," said my father to the soldier. "You've got a proper young lady here." Summoner Bradford was a man to be listened to, as there was power in his quiet way.

I couldn't sleep a bit for the singing and smells of cigars, rancid ham and coal smoke from the engine wafting through the train cars; waves of lilac perfume from a passing young woman decked out in scarlet velvet with a low, low bodice showing more than its share of milky white skin.     A soldier whistled long and low, reaching out his foot to trip her skirts up. She just sneered at his boldness and kept walking. Her high leather boots had gleaming pearl buttons. The ivory handle of a knife peeked out from one of them. Her eyes darted around the rows of soldiers. She passed a card to one of them over my head. I snuck a peek.

**Mrs. Ella Stewart's Comfort House. 12$^{th}$ and Pennsylvania,** it read.

The soldier snickered and passed the card down the row of his comrades.

As the watch-fires of the soldier's camps that ringed the forts surrounding Washington City came into view—more lights than I'd ever seen in my life, glowing like Christmas candles through a smoky fog—cheers and shouts went up from the soldiers: *Huzzah! Down with the Rebs! Praise Glory! We're coming, Mr. Lincoln!*

The train engine wheezed, then lurched to a stop. "Washington City!" cried the conductor. There was bumping and jostling as men piled into the aisles. I stood up and looked back at the soldiers, the ones still sitting. One had a milk-cow's calm liquid gaze. Another sat trembling in his seat, eying the darkness through the window. We had come for the war. Or had it come for us?

Three

We took a carriage from the B&O train depot deep into the capitol city. Even though it was late at night, the streets were crowded and noisy. I could make out wagons pulled by huge Clydesdale horses, fancy black carriages lit by candles in domes of glass, and a group of chained Negroes dragged along by a man riding a horse and cracking a whip.

"My God." Papa said softly, clenching his fists. "If I ever doubted why I am in this war . . . "

"That there is Murder Bay," said our driver, an old gray-haired Negro man with a battered gray cloth hat and a worn black suit with white lapels. "Folks don't want to have no truck with that place. Yonder is the Center Market. Food so fine and meat so pump and shiny a body could fatten itself just looking at it."

We drove past huge houses, marbled and dormered with rows of black, shiny carriages stopped at tall, iron gates, flooded by gas lamps. Past open fields of high grasses, soldier's tents, and lines of mules and cattle, their heads and manes barely visible in the darkness.

Smells, so many of them: Horse manure, baking bread, rotted meat, fire smoke, coal tar, and burning wood.

The driver told us that my Aunt Salome's house was just two city blocks from the President's Park.

"Mr. Lincoln's White House is there. So are the War Department, the Navy Department, and the Treasury. You are in the belly of things," he said, with a low whistle. "Yes suh, you are in the belly. And I pray you Godspeed, as I seen by that uniform that you are in Mr. Lincoln's army."

"Indeed I am," my father said. "And proud to be."

It was past midnight when we finally approached the front steps of Aunt Salome Hutton's boardinghouse at 1240 Sixteenth Street. It was on a tree-lined, quiet block, one of a row of houses made of wood and brick with narrow stone stairs leading to the front door.

Just then I saw a man scurry away from behind the house. He was tall, and very dark-skinned; I could make out no features at all in the shadow. He had a gun, the butt of it just visible in a sliver of shine caught by a tremor of moonlight. He turned his head this way and that like a hawk spotting prey or a hunter. He ducked away into an alley.        "A runaway, I'll wager," the driver whispered, a look of sadness on his face.

I thought of Mr. Amos Jefferson, the blacksmith's assistant in our village who Mama said used to be a slave. He was always on the lookout for the slave-catchers, even in faraway New Hampshire. I saw whip scars down his back and arms.

Mama told me Mr. Jefferson's family had been sold away down to a plantation in the south and that he'd never see them again. After my accident, on one of our rare trips to town, Mr. Amos Jefferson thanked Mama and Papa for warning him that some strange men were prowling around the village. After that, my parents put Mr. Jefferson up in an abandoned barn behind our cabin until the slave catchers were gone. That act did not go down so well with many of the town elders. Being kind to some Negroes was one thing, sheltering them was quite another. They liked their world just as it was: White, and unchanged, and whiter again, with everyone in their place.

I remember kneeling down and praying for Amos Jefferson right there in the ice cream parlor, between the jars of chocolate bits and the jellybeans. Then I counted the beans out loud.

"She's passing strange, that one." One lady said to another who was licking the last bit of butterscotch syrup from the bottom of her dish. "The child is hexed," the other said. "And her shabby parents are Negro lovers, to boot." No wonder I hated going to the village.

I was remembering the taste of the awful pink liquid the doctor gave me to 'make me right again,' a sure cure for brain sickness he'd said, when the carriage rolled to a stop. The air in Washington City was hot and still, with no scent of the sea at all.

"I can't breathe here, Papa," I said, my shoulders sagging and my arms hurting as I helped my father lug our traveling trunk to the front door.     Before my father could reach up to ring the brass bell that hung from a rope, the door opened. A faded, older woman in a nightcap stood there with her hands folded across her chest and a scowl on her face.

"Devilish time to appear, Summoner," she said, pursing her lips. Papa's full name was Summoner Elias Bradford, but Mama had called him "Sum."

"I'm sorry about the late hour, Salome," my father said, lifting my trunk.

"I have a servant for that," she snapped. Gray-streaked tendrils of hair like limp spider legs dangled to her shawl.

"Nellie, Nellie!" she yelled. "Get out from the privy and help my brother and this child."

"I'm not a child," I muttered.

"Yes, Missus Salome." A large Negro woman walked past her out the door.

"Sorry, missus," She said to my aunt as she dragged our trunk to the darkened entryway, "my innards was galled and all."     "Lazy and sick, what good are you then?" My aunt said, putting her hand on my head.

"She's tall, this girl." She whisked off my cloak and glanced down at my droopy mourning dress. "I hope she brought some decent, light colored clothing."

19

And as an afterthought, she muttered, "Oh, the black dress, of course, Summoner, I'd forgotten about your wife's passing. I'm sorry about, uh, Joanie."

"Jenny!" I yelled. "Her name was Jenny! Jenny Aurelia O'Dell Bradford!" Papa grabbed my arm. "Hush up."

I felt so angry that his sister didn't even know Mama's name that I felt like racing out into the night, then and there. I glowered, my head down.

"She must have left her manners on the train, eh?" my aunt said.

I was so tired, and so overwhelmed at the thought of staying with this cold aunt of mine, that I swayed and almost fainted.

"Summoner! This child is near a swoon." My aunt pulled me through the hall into a big kitchen with a cook stove piled with pots and skillets, all under a wide fire. Nellie was wiping sweat from her face with a red and yellow patterned kerchief. She was murmuring softly to a chicken that was nibbling cracked corn from her hand.          "That's supper, not a pet, am I right?" Aunt Salome scolded. "Of course I am. And Nellie! Biscuits and beef in a hurry. This child is near passed out from hunger."   "I'm not a child," I said again, standing as straight as I could in spite of an aching in my bones.  Aunt Salome scowled at me. "Well excuse me then, Miss Sassy."

My father shushed me again. "Madeline is fifteen, Salome," he said.

"And still growing, I expect. Does she eat a lot?" my aunt asked, feeling my ribs.  "Ain't got no biscuits, missus; they won't be none 'til morning," Nellie said. With that, she plucked a slab of beef from the serving plate, slathered it with juices, and peered hard at me. "Eat, Miss," she said, holding out the same to my father. Her eyes were grave, a mellow golden-brown, with a broad, flared-nostril African nose. She carried herself proudly, in spite of her station.

"Thank you, ma'am," my father said.

"All right then, suh," Nellie answered, backing away, as though his respect-ful tone scorched her. "Thank you, suh." She reached into the chicken's cage, stroked hits head once, and twisted its neck really fast. The dying chicken flopped and flapped around until it landed on my foot. I started sobbing, and heading for the door.  Sure I'd seen chickens killed before, but that night, the sight of the poor bird made all my sadness burst out.

My father followed me, trying to wipe away my tears with his hand.

But as though my tears were just a passing rain shower and with no words of comfort at all, my aunt showed us to our room.

"I'll leave you to your rest," she said, handing me a handkerchief. "Put it in the laundry pile after you've used it. I've got to go pick up all the cushions in the parlor. Seems I've lost my wedding band, and Lord knows my departed husband paid a good sum for it."

"It's by the hat stand, just to the left of the big plant," I said, blowing my nose really loudly … on purpose.

"What? Where is it, and how . . .?" My aunt's mouth hung open.

"I saw a glint of gold as we were coming upstairs, ma' am. If you look, you'll find it there."

My father stared straight ahead. Maybe he was waiting for me to say just how many flowers there were on my aunt's faded rose wallpaper, or have another burst of crying. I didn't say anything more. I knew better.

"Thank you," my aunt said stiffly. "I hope you are right. I was going to look for the ring in Nellie's room, just off the kitchen. I thought maybe she filched it, not that she's tried anything crafty like that before, but you know how they can be."

"We *don't* know," my father said. "Nellie seems a fine woman. Goodnight, Salome."

"I do declare," my aunt muttered over and over as she bustled off.

"There are forty-six roses on each wall," I said. "Now let's get out of here, Papa."

He just sighed and I silently unpacked my things; the buttercup yellow chemise Mama made me, a linsey-woolsey day dress, my favorite coveralls I wore most every day, two woolen work-shirts, a straw hat, and a handkerchief that belonged to Mama, her sweet scent; lilacs and summer rain, still on it. I held it to my face, inhaling the last of her.

"We have to let her go, Maddie." Papa said softly as he traced his finger across a sampler Mama finished on one of her better days. On it a little girl with brown braids stood waist high in tall summer grass, nubbins of thread making freckles on her face. She was pointing at the sky. On the bottom Mama had written *My Madeline*, and the year, *1857*. Papa put it on the dresser, and closing the trunk containing his belongings with a thud and a snap of the latch. "Jenny," He whispered.

Papa had tears in his eyes. I'd cried so hard earlier mine were nearly swollen shut.

"We'll make it through, Maddie. Somehow. Find your strength." Papa curled up in a big, overstuffed chair, and I fell exhausted into a small spindle bed. My feet hung over the end.

The last thing I remember before sleep finally came was Nellie's chicken, struggling to right itself and run away.

Four

Raucous cries of "knives for the lady! Pots fine! Rags and bones, ashes too!" jolted me awake. I peeked through the window over my bed and saw a crush of carts and carriages, mules and soldiers all massed in the street below. I thought about our tiny, quiet cabin on the riverbank and mama dancing like a fairy princess in a patch of sunlight on the grass.

I splashed water on my face and tried to run a comb through my tangles of hair. I saw two dresses lying across the chair in my room. One was a pale yellow homespun with a high white collar and a wide skirt. The other was a lightweight spring frock, faded brownish, sewn by a careless hand, uneven stitches up the bodice and down the front. A stiff petticoat and a small hoop with metal scaffolding sat like a collapsed pumpkin beside it. A corset with cotton laces, a pair of scratched leather high button boots, a tan porkpie hat and green bonnet completed my new wardrobe. My black dress and stockings were jammed into the drawer of an old wooden wardrobe. That was okay. I never wanted to see them again. I hated wearing black for mama. She was all brightness, like my own sun.

But I guessed—rightly, I might add—that even though it sounded like I'd be a mere scullery maid in that house, Aunt Salome wanted me to look like something resembling a lady.

My father was still sleeping. I gave him a quick kiss on the forehead and went behind a tattered dressing screen to change out of my high-necked sleeping gown into my clothes.

I put on the yellow dress, the petticoat and hoop skirt, that was too short for me. I'd never worn such garb back in Portsmouth. Mama said hoops made folks look like they might tip over in a light wind.

"Besides, darling, "she'd say, in her lilting Irish brogue, "the mark of a fine lady lies not in her hoops, but in her manner and mind."

I peeked at myself in a looking glass that hung on the wall. The color made my face pale, and my freckles looked like deep brown dots rampaging across my nose. The boots pinched my feet worse than my black, scuffed up ones. I sighed, and like a sailing craft pitching on a rough sea, I went to find my aunt.

Her boardinghouse had three stories and ten rooms: An entrance parlor, six bedrooms and a sewing room. Of course, Nellie's room was the tiniest just off the kitchen. There was a small door I'd seen when Papa and I were there I imagined led to a cellar.

The furnishings were a hodge-podge of white, wooden chairs and tables, two old mahogany buffets, and an assortment of over-stuffed divans backed with tattered lace. Paintings of plump cows hung next to biblical scenes of Jesus on the cross, and devils wielding pitchforks at frightened children.

23

I went back upstairs, and found my aunt having a cup of tea in the parlor. A hat stand with carved lions' heads loomed over her.

"Thank you for the clothes, Aunt Salome." I said, not meaning a word of it.

"We dress respectable here," she said, watching as I tipped forward in the stupid skirt nearly upending a table full of knick-knacks.

"And try not to topple over, Madeline."

My aunt held out a blue-veined, long-fingered hand. "See, I did find my ring. It was just where you said. My dear departed husband would offer a thank-you. But I thought it was mighty peculiar that you noticed it at all. By the way, I lock my money in a safe."

Did she mean she was suspicious of me because I found her darn ring? I should have kept that to myself!

"Now, give Nellie a hand with the wood for the dining room hearth."

While I was helping drag logs from the alley to the kitchen, and I sure didn't need to wear that awful yellow dress to do that, I spotted a newspaper lying on the ground. It was the *New York Tribune.* After I'd cracked eggs and put bacon on the iron skillet, I laid the paper on the chopping block and read. Aunt Salome came up behind me, yanking most of the paper from my hand.

"Those Yankee papers burn well," she muttered, crumpling them up and throwing them on the floor. She rang a rusty bell by the door.

"Nellie! Come clean up. Can't have folks think we live in a slave cabin, all littered and filthy." When she'd gone, I grabbed up a page of the newspaper and began to read quickly. There were headlines about all the troops arriving in the city to repel a Confederate invasion, if necessary. Down the page was a particular column that caught my eye. It seemed to be written like someone was talking, not the usual reporting of numbers of soldiers or the puffed-up talk of politicians. It was the voice of a stranger in a strange place, just like me.

I've copied out all of these special dispatches throughout my story. You'll see why. Here is the first one I read:

*New York Tribune*Special dispatch from Washington City

**I am alone here in a city like no other, in a time like no other, where an Illinois justice seeker named Lincoln leads our nation in a war like no other. I'm a young stranger in a capitol brimming with chaos.**

**Where I settle must remain anonymous, as must I. Even though *On to Richmond!* is the call heard all around, and though many, including this reporter, think it is premature to urge unseasoned troops forward, I am here to swear the South must be defeated, for the slaver still auctions and the slave is still sold. That is what Mr. Greeley, the publisher of this fine paper, believes as well. But many here do not.**

**As it is a time when supposed traitors, scoundrels, and plotters are locked tight in prison, I ask this: What is loyalty? Is one man's patriot another man's traitor? Will brother face brother, each willing to die for a cause they believe in?**

**I am here to find out.**

**So I will roam and use the wondrous new telegraph machine known as "The Lightning" to send my dispatches back to my paper.**

**I sign herein, and forever after as**

**PAN**

           *     I slipped the page into my bodice, feeling pity for the writer who called himself PAN—a name I remembered from Greek mythology, a god of shepherds and wind. Or was it pity for myself, knowing my father would be leaving that very day?

"Mrs. Salome don't take kindly to reading business from the outside, Miss," Nellie said. "Except her holy scriptures, the *Washington Intelligencer* where she puts in her ads for boarders, and the paper that favors the Rebels: the *New York Herald*. You got that?"

"Yes," I answered, somehow knowing I would find and read those *Tribune* dispatches whenever they appeared.

I clutched my father's hand at the breakfast table. The thought of his departure was making it hard to swallow. The johnnycakes and bacon stuck in my throat as Aunt Salome introduced us to her one boarder, a very old man called The Colonel, who had long, wispy white hair. He held his fork with a trembling hand. Clutched in his other was a small revolver. He pointed it at my father in his uniform and whispered, "traitor."

"We're not enemies at this table, sir," my father said, reaching over and gently removing the gun from the old man's hand. I noticed a tiny Confederate flag on the Colonel's lapel.

The Colonel opened his mouth but only hissing sounds came from his throat. All his teeth but one were missing. He grabbed my hand and pressed it to his dry lips.

Then, the poor man's head fell forward and crashed into a china tureen that held the remaining eggs. His hands were limp.

"Oh, Lord, my good china!" Aunt Salome picked up the cracked tureen, cradling the pieces in her hands. The Colonel lay still.

"Nellie!" my aunt shouted. "Come get the Colonel."

Nellie bustled in and, lifting the old man in her arms like he weighed nothing, and carried him upstairs.

"Usually he faints away *after* the table is cleared," my aunt said, shaking her head disapprovingly and mopping up the spilled eggs with a napkin.

The meal went on as though nothing had happened. I felt like I was going to scream. I stood up.

"Remain at table, Madeline," my aunt ordered. My father pulled me back down to my seat.

Nellie came to the table, a pitcher of milk in her hand. "I'm afeered the Colonel has passed on, Missus Salome," she said.

My father got up from the table.

"Shall I help with the body?"

"No, sir, I got hold of it," Nellie said. "I'll wash him up so when the cemetery cart come, he'll be fit to meet Jesus sure."

Just as I was saying a silent prayer for the Colonel, the door to the dining room opened. A young man walked, or rather limped, to the table at a tilt, as though blown sideways. He was tall and burly, with a shock of black hair that curled about his starched collar. "Last to come, Mr. Whitestone. Was your sleep disturbed?" Aunt Salome asked, an unusual note of kindness in her voice. "Yes, ma'am. The newness of it all, I suppose," he said, shooting a quick glance around the table, his eyes resting lastly on me. He had bright green eyes, a strong chin with a cleft in the middle, and suddenly, my cheeks were burning hot. I reached for a tumbler of water, accidentally spilling it over the tablecloth, and wiping clumsily at the puddle. "Sorry," I said, looking down at the pooling liquid.

Aunt Salome forced a smile, "It's only water, not blood." This comment brought another rusty chuckle to her throat. Jake Whitestone's eyes met mine. He was hiding a smile behind his napkin.

I looked away. My cheeks burned. What was happening to me?

"Madeline! You'll starve to a rail," Aunt Salome snapped, shoving my plate even closer.

My father whispered, "Just to please her, take some bites, Maddie. I have to go now. My camp isn't far. I'll come back soon." He whispered again, "I'm leaving the Colonel's revolver in your trunk upstairs, Madeline. The war, it seems, is all around us." Good, I thought. Papa had taught me to shoot and I was good at it. *As long as you don't kill a living thing, Maddie, he'd said when we were deep in the forest as I shot at rocks lining an ancient, crumbling wall.*

My father got up from the table, straightened his uniform jacket, and headed for the door. "Thank you, Salome," he said, "for taking care of my precious Maddie."

My aunt nodded. "Godspeed, brother," she said, rubbing her eyes. Was she about to cry, the hard old thing? "Don't worry over her, hear?"

My breakfast came up in my throat. I jumped up from the table and fled toward the kitchen, nearly toppling Nellie as she struggled through the door with a huge bowl of applesauce. I knelt down, my breath coming in gasps. I was heaving, but nothing came up. Saying goodbye to my father filled me with dread.

Behind me, I heard the dragging of one foot behind the other, like someone was limping. It was Mr. Whitestone.

"My I offer some assistance, miss?"

I didn't answer. I just kept staring at the floor.

"It's hard saying goodbye, isn't it?" He knelt down next to me.

I looked away. "What do you know about it?" I snapped, my voice gruff and low.

How could he know what I was feeling, or what was hard for me?

I stood up to get away, but I was unsteady on my feet, and I fell right against Mr. Whitestone. I jerked away as though I'd been stung by a bee. I stepped clear of him.

"You don't know anything about us," I whispered.

"That's true," he said. "But I know this. Your father is in Mr. Lincoln's army. My father is a Rebel."

I was listening, then. I finally looked at Mr. Whitestone. His face was so sad.

"Your father is true to the cause and willing to die for it. Be grateful," he said, giving a little bow to me, and leaving by a small side door that I later learned led to a street through the alley.

I was stunned and confused. What was Mr. Whitestone doing here? Did his bad leg keep him out of the war? Was he a coward, or maybe he was a rebel like his father. It seemed like everyone was suspicious. Oh, how I wished Papa were there, so I could talk to him about all this.

Through that same window, I watched him mount a horse and ride away. I wanted to race out and tell him how much I loved him, but I just stood there, wishing like crazy that I could go with him.

*Wishes are fishes. You are here now. Heaven help you.*

To fight away my sadness, I fixed my mind on the young man I'd just met. Was I a gibbering mess because he was so handsome? Bosh!

*

I opened the door, not to follow Jake Whitestone or my father, mind you, but to get some air, and untangle my brain. Although I didn't realize it then, I started spying when I was there in that alley. I found myself out in a high-walled enclosure with broken cobblestones, a tangle of thorny vines and rambling ivy-covered brick walls. A rat skittered between my feet; a crow, something large and shiny in its beak swooped overhead and then, I heard voices. Loud voices from afar, like after I had my accident and every sound was turned up.

"Man up, private, and stop your blubbering!" a man said.

"Jeez, I want my mama," another cried out.

27

"Man up. Fool! We muster in the morning."

I looked all around me. I was alone in the alley.

I couldn't see beyond the walls, so I headed toward an opening at the end of the alley. I stepped into the street and was nearly run down by a newsboy racing ahead of a milk wagon.

"Extra!" the boy shouted. "The Rebels march in Virginia! Might Washington City Fall?"

I stood gaping at five soldiers across the road. They were laughing and stumbling, dragging a weeping man by the collar.

"Mama, Mama!" he sobbed. "I don't want to die."

I'd heard his voice all the way back in the alley, I realized.

One of the soldiers stopped when he saw me and beckoned me to come closer.

"Whoo-ee! Come to me, sweet thing!" he said with a leer on his face.

I looked him in the eye like he was a wild boar in the woods, steady and hard, without blinking.

"Excuse me, miss," he said, backing away.

A Negro woman with a wash-basket on her head deftly swerved between the drunken soldiers. She was very, very tall, with a brightly striped yellow and red bandana around her neck. Or was it a woman? There was something strange about her. Somehow, she moved like a man.

I stepped further into the street. I didn't get far. A strong hand grasped my elbow. I whipped around to see who was there. It was Nellie, her face set in a scowl. She wrapped my arm firmly in hers. "Bad sorts, Miss, that's what's out there." She steered me back though the alley toward the boardinghouse door and into the kitchen.

"You set right down. I'm making a pineapple upside down cake. Seeing as you is just that, upside down, I'm meaning, maybe you'll have a bit and you'll be right-ways."

She stretched a quilt with blue criss-crosses and a steamboat wheel embroidered on it over the top of a window glass on the door.    "Now you won't be peering out to them sorry sights," she said.

"I was just taking it all in." I said, and told her exactly what I'd seen; the soldiers, the washerwoman, everything.

"You caught all this in the wink of time you was out?" she said, shelling her peas so fast that a bunch fell to the floor.    "I remember things," was all I answered.

"Umm-hum," Nellie murmured, a worried look on her face.

"Do you have any family, Nellie?" I asked, hoping she wasn't alone here in this hard city.

She dumped the peas into a heavy pot and hung it over the fire.

"Just my son, Isaac," she said, glancing down.

"Does he work for my aunt, too?"

With one hand Nellie poured water from a pitcher; with the other she wiped her brow on her bandana. It was the same color and pattern the washerwoman in the alley was wearing.

"Isaac ain't in these parts. Got to set the waiter out to boil. Then them ham hocks, see, goes on top." Nellie kicked up the fire under the pot with a poker.

I handed her the plate of ham parts.

"That door, with the heavy latch, where does it go?" I asked, pointing to the small door the back of the kitchen.

"That goes to the cellar, right, Nellie?"

"It goes nowhere, nowhere," she said, her voice raised. "There's bugs and spirit-devils down there, so stay clear of it."

Of course I decided then and there to explore it if I could.

There was a small, scraping sound outside the alley door. Just then, Nellie doused the lamp that lit our small corner of the dark kitchen.    "Get on with you now, miss," she said, getting all firm again, taking my arm and steering me from the room.

"Is something wrong, Nellie?" Her complete change of mood and her sudden dousing of the lamp shocked me.

"Miss Madeline, leave me now! Git!" Nellie picked up a rolling pin, and moved toward the door. She brandished the wooden roller like it was a weapon.

*

It was the letter from my father the next day that fixed me in a plan.

*Maddie-mine,* he said, *I'm settling in, and oh, my daughter, I hope you are all right and minding your aunt.*

*My camp is like an Eden lying in a sprawl of oaks and pines on the grounds of a mansion owned by a Mr. Gales. It is about four miles from where you are now, so I'm hoping to get a pass to see you real soon. I promise.*

*There are some good fellows here.*

*I've never been in close company with men, and truth, Maddie, I like it fine. But I sure am itching to fight.*

*Keep me and Mama in your heart. Remember we're always with you. Love, and love again,*

*Papa*

I found a map of the city in my aunt's parlor and memorized it. I saw just where he was, out on Bladensburg Road, right before the Maryland border, and the street route that took him there. I decided to find him, and join him no matter what.

How? How would I do it? I felt like a fox caught in a snare, ready to chew its own paw off to be free.

But when the mysterious man came to stay at the boarding house, the trap that held me opened. A hole just big enough for me to crawl through appeared until finally, I made my escape.

## Five

He bowed, removed a wide-brimmed white hat, and seated himself at the table. He was decked out in a white linen suit with a narrow, dark brown tie.

"I'm Timothy Webster," he said.

Aunt Salome rose up slowly like she was a queen—and actually curtsied! How phony and dumb did that look?

"I've just arrived in the city, madam, from the faraway Carolinas."    Mr. Webster spoke with a pronounced southern accent, dragging out syllables and dropping the ends of words. He was of middle size and of middling age, maybe in his thirties, it was hard to tell. He was stocky, with large, strong hands, a heavy beard and moustache that twirled up like half moons at its two waxy ends, and a thatch of black hair salted with gray. His left pinky was bent over like a gnarled apple tree branch.

"I saw your notice of rooms to let, Mrs. Hutton, and, well, here I am," he said. Aunt Salome fanned herself with a napkin and simpered.

Mr. Webster smiled at me. "What is your name, young miss?" he asked. His iron-gray eyes looked straight into mine, as though he could see into my brain. But his manner was so gentle, and his voice so musical, I was not uncomfortable. I forgot for an instant that he was likely a Rebel.

"I'm Madeline Eve Bradford," I said softly.

"Her father wears Union Blue," Salome said, as though describing a disease.

"She's here for, well, for the duration of our little conflict," she added.

*Little conflict? It was a darn war! And just wait, I'm going to find a way to be part of it.*

"Will you be taking all your meals with us, sir?" My aunt sighed. "Some don't pay for their board," she said, with a sideways glance to me, "so your fine greenbacks, sir, are as welcome as the sun."

My face reddened at this humiliation. "Nellie!" she shouted. "Go find another chicken for supper, and don't be making of pet of it this time."

I winced.

"Yes, missus," Nellie answered from behind the door.

"Well, then, well, Mr. Webster," asked Aunt Salome sweetly, "Is cotton your trade?"    "Brilliant as well as handsome you are, madam," Webster answered, bowing his head. "King Cotton is my master, and I am its humble slave, no matter what the outcome of your 'little war.'"

By then, Jake Whitestone had seated himself at the table, looking mussed and gray-faced, with dark circles under his eyes, tousled and weary like he'd been out all night. *Where had he been, and why did I care? I'd be gone.*

Before I left the room, I pushed my uneaten breakfast plate under Jake Whitestone's nose. He reached for my arm.

"Miss Bradford, I have to talk to you. May we be excused, Mrs. Hutton?"

"Well, I never," Aunt Salome huffed.

I followed Jake Whitestone into the kitchen.

The words rushed out of him in a whisper.

"Your father's regiment will march to Centreville, Virginia, Miss Bradford. General Burnside has it that the Rebels are on the move, and our troops are to face them front-on. If all this information is right, they'll meet up with General McDowell and save Washington City from an invasion. It will end it."       "How do you know this?" I asked.

"I overheard … things."

"Madeline?" My aunt called out. "Did a regiment snatch you up, or are you loitering?"

"Good day, Mr. Whitestone."

Before he could speak, I was gone.

*

*Almost, almost.* As I was getting some things from the alleyway, Holding a candle and rummaging through a waste bin, actually, I noticed a rolled up newspaper just by the door. I scanned it quickly as I waited for the house to be dead dark, for them all to be asleep.

**Special from the *New York Tribune***

**Dear Readers,**

**Our soldiers under General Irvin McDowell are on the move to meet the Rebel General Beauregard's Confederate Army at a location that must remain unknown. For now.**

**Both sides are green and untried, boys and men who, like the sunshine patriots of our great Revolution, have heard a bell tolling, summoning them to war. Your reporter is on the move as well. In a great hurry, I might add. I aim to find the battle, and see it for myself.**

**I telegraph in haste. PAN**

It was beginning! Whoever the writer was, I envied his freedom to move about as no proper woman could. No *woman*, that is.

## Six

When the faint light of dawn shimmered at the edge of blackness, I grabbed up my things and ran through the alley. In an oversized, brown topcoat trimmed in straggled beaver fur, and dirty yellow striped pants, I figured I'd pass for a boy or a raging lunatic. It didn't matter, then. Out, I was out. My hair was tucked up under a fawn-colored top hat and pulled low over my face. In my mouth was a cigar, thin, small, and unlit. Jammed down in my oversized boot was the old Colonel's loaded revolver my father had given me.

Before I left, I stamped down hard on the miserable hoop that held out my skirt, crushed it to pieces and dumped it in the refuse bin. The rest of the clothes, well, I'd pilfered them. The boots were left in the alley, along with the colonel's clothes. Aunt Salome had pitched the poor old man's things into a barrel of torn, dirty kitchen rags. There they'd sat, a mournful heap meant for the rubbish man and his wheezy old horse, until I had pulled them out.    Smelling like old mutton and moldy rags, I moved along, hips forward in imitation of a man's long stride, and a mighty aching in my feet, as I'd stuffed the oversized boots with bits of old newspaper.

Like Nellie and my aunt said, no young girl could ever go about unescorted in a city like this with all manner of hucksters, bawdy women, soldiers, and bummers of every ilk and stripe. Bosh! I focused hard on the map in my head.

I made my way from my aunt's house up along Sixteenth Street to Pennsylvania Avenue. In the distance, I saw the white porticos and rolling green lawn that surrounded the President's House. A phalanx of armed soldiers walked back and forth in front of the wrought iron fence. I vowed to have a closer look when I could but the image of my father's face made me move faster.

I crossed over the avenue, barely avoiding a rush of gilded carriages and one -horse carts. I turned right on New York Avenue. I'd have to walk along this road for a good mile or so as it passed straight up to North Capitol Street, not far from my father's camp. Packed cheek to jowl were tumbledown wooden houses with child-crowded doorways and mangy dogs darting every which way, snarling and snapping as they tore at bones. "Oysters! Pearly as dawn, fresh as a maiden's kiss!" cried a vendor in a filthy apron with scratches over his hands. The white sea-flesh peeked from the shells, a sure sign the oysters were not in any way fresh; this I well knew. When a dog approached the oyster cart, the man heaved a broken shell at its head.   I slipped in a puddle of oyster water and heaven knows what else, my cigar falling smack into the mess, my hair nearly tumbling from under my hat. Just then, a heavy booted soldier who reeked of alcohol jostled me hard.    "Watch your way, son," he said, and swore an oath under his breath I dare not repeat. He kicked aside a pair of pigs snuffling in the dirt. Son! He called me son. Praise be, I'd fooled him, even if he was dead drunk, just then pitching forward on his face.

I walked faster, dodging an omnibus pulled by two heaving dray horses, and a closed carriage with high-stepping, glistening bays, finally crossing over toward the middle of New York Avenue, near to K Street, a sedate block lined with brass railed fences and hitching posts, an occasional Negro servant emptying a pail of slops in the side yards—three, to be exact.

The sun was out and blazing. A moist, suffocating heat pressed in on me. My clothing itched, my boots blistered my feet, and my face dripped perspiration clear down my collar. I had to pause to rest.

Moments before, I'd passed an alleyway that ran behind the street. I walked back to it, and yes, there was shade, and some small coolness. I stepped into the alley past a refuse bin full of fruit peels, bottles, and a pile of stinking manure-covered hay. I paused there, wiping my face with my sleeve.

I'd just removed my jacket when a tall, blonde slender young woman passed, her bright hair caught up in a chignon that sat low on her neck. She wore a creamy satin gown with a lace collar fastened with a cameo brooch. She walked slowly into the alley, stopping just a few feet way from me. I pressed myself to the wall so I'd be hidden from her view.

She pulled a small pistol from a pearl-studded purse that hung on her waist. I crouched down low in a space just between the woodpile and the wall and watched her as she paced this way and that, looking, watching; waiting.

In moments, a mustachioed man walked toward her. He was slim and ele-gantly dressed in a tan-colored linen suit and spotless brown boots. He strode up to the girl. He, too, had a weapon, a bright silver long-barreled gun. I crouched lower, folding myself further into the space.

"The way is clear, Colonel Jordan," Her voice was like a purr, soft and southern-accented. He turned in a full circle, his hand on the gun.

"I said we're alone, didn't I?" Then slowly, carefully, she unpinned her chi-gnon. Coils of hair, a shower of bright gold fell to her waist. The man pocketed his gun and moved closer to her. Before I looked away, thinking I might see something no young girl should be privy to, he ran his hands through her tresses, caressing each strand, finally, closing his fingers around something, flat and tiny—a flat packet. He unrolled a paper inside and smiled.

"Miss Duvall, we thank you," he said, kissing her hand. "Our brave Betty Duvall." They stood very close together. He touched her face.

The girl took his hand. "It is the least I can do, sir."

"Mrs. Greenhow will have another dispatch for you presently," he said. "The Yankees are ready to move. At her command, ride east at sunset. I'll meet you at Centreville. I'm on my way now."

She nodded. "God save the South."

"God save the South," he answered, like he was saying a prayer. He slipped the packet into his left pocket, pulled his gun from the right one, and walked quickly through the alley in the opposite direction from where I was hidden. I had no choice but to stay put as the girl he called Betty Duvall quickly pinned up her hair, patting the whole of it smooth. With a blazing smile on her face, she flounced back to the street.

When Colonel Jordan was far enough away, his back still to me, I crawled from the woodpile, out of the alley and into the street, nearly colliding with a man in a long black coat and a white collar—clerical garb. A squat black hat was pulled down low on his head.

"Beg pardon, my dear," he said, in a heavily accented foreign voice. A group of ragged Negroes struggling with huge wooden timbers low on their backs blocked my way as I tried to cross to the other side. The clergyman stood at the street corner. He waved a Bible at soldiers as they passed.

"Save your souls before battle! Read your holy book! It doesn't take sides," he yelled. There was something odd, something familiar about him that held my eye, but I was so intent on following the girl called Betty I kept moving.

Finally I got to the other side of the street. As I craned my neck to see if I could catch another glimpse of her, a butcher with lamb and pig carcasses slung over his shoulders elbowed me aside.

Then I saw Betty Duvall approaching one of the houses I'd just passed, a three-story brick townhouse at 1625 K. Street, to be exact. She sashayed through a line of soldiers standing guard outside, climbed the stairs, and rapped on the door. It opened quickly. In the entryway stood another woman, regal of stance. Her up-swept hair was copper-bright. I moved closer to hear what they were saying.

I noticed that nearly hidden by the volume of the woman's full skirts was a small girl-child twirling a doll. As the child lifted the doll, I saw it had on a blue petticoat with lace trim.

"My dear Amanda," I heard the woman speak loudly to the girl I'd just heard called Betty, "My little Rose and I have waited a long while for you. My darling daughter adores the new doll clothes you sent!"

After the door closed, I watched the little girl part the curtains, and prop the doll in the window. It looked to be the same one I'd seen, but in place of the blue checked petticoat was one of yellow.

"Who lives in that house?" I blurted my question to one of the soldiers standing close by. I was testing my lowest man-like voice.

"Say what?" he said. "Speak up!"

I lowered my voice even more. "Who lives there?"

"Ain't you a curious hayfoot! That's that infernal Rebel Rose Greenhow's place." He nudged me in the ribs. "She's the worst kind of traitor. She gives her favors to both sides, and manages to get out Rebel messages right under the noses of the detectives tasked to keep her under watch." He gave me another nudge with his elbow, laughing lewdly. "Maybe she'll take a shine to you."

I quickly nudged him back and gave a knowing chuckle that sounded more like a gargle.

"She'll pay for her ways, surely, I'll warrant," the other soldier said. "All those traitors will pay." He spit a stream of tobacco into the street. "See, that Bible toter there might be one of her watchers," he said, motioning to the clergyman I'd just seen.

I must have looked really puzzled. "Watcher?" I asked.

"A detective—a Pinkerton man, dunderhead. They keep an eye on her in plain sight so they can catch her at her treason. Didn't I already say that? Or are you some Rebel snitch?" He pushed me. "Move on now, vagrant, or we'll ship you off to the calaboose."

"Yes, sir," I said. Before I left, I took another look at the clergyman. There was something about him. What was it? Sure, he wore a cleric's collar and was gripping the Bible, with . . . Yes! That was it. One crooked pinky finger rested on an open page. I squinted hard to see his face. I couldn't, but I saw a gray-streaked beard, and then it came to me. I knew just who he was! It was our boarder Timothy Webster, I was sure of it!

Could he be a Pinkerton detective, like the soldier said? Mr. Webster told us he was a Rebel cotton trader when he came to the boardinghouse.

But I'd dallied too long. No time to ponder all I'd seen, though I knew I'd remember every detail. I had to get to my father—in one piece.

I ran fast along New York Avenue until it met North Capitol Street. Remember, I told myself; there was a shortcut, a pathway. Yes! There it was. I stumbled through a clump of willow trees toward a vine-covered footbridge leading to a tow-path along the Potomac River. The water was brackish, a black sheen smeared like petroleum oil atop it. The river smelled of decay, and no wonder, as a horse's corpse floated by, its belly bloated and the ears half eaten off by many a passing fish. I trekked farther, so tired now I was almost fainting. I'd walked at least three miles. I kept going along to a narrow walkway overhung with moss-covered trees. I knew this would lead straight to the grounds of the Eckington Hospital and my father's camp.     I'd been walking a good while longer when at last I spied rows of whitewashed wooden buildings nested on a sprawling lawn of bright, green grass. Just beyond them were brown tents, cook fires, and crowds of soldiers as far as I could see. Like water beetles they scurried about, piling mules with packs, dragging cannons, their voices muted. I knew my father's fine regiment would be armed with breech loading Sharp's rifles, stick-like, but holding a mighty power.

"Halt! Not another step." Three armed soldiers flanked me, moving me forward in a ragged two-step, finally stopping at a new, wooden gate.

"Pass?" One of the soldiers demanded, his voice hard. "What?" I winced.

"Pass! Or you can't go any further." "State your name and business, uh . . ."—one of them scanned me from head to toe—"sir." I had to think fast. Who was I? "Looks like he's got up in something passing strange," another soldier said. "Smells like the dickens, too." "I have a message for—" "What? Speak up, son."

My voice was cracking. "Yes, sirs, I need to see Private Summoner Bradford of the 2$^{nd}$ New Hampshire. Urgently." "You don't say?" "I don't say what?" I whispered. They moved closer. The largest loomed over me. "What is your business with him? I won't need to ask again, will I?" "His daughter is dying!" I blurted out. I tried to push past them. I was shoved hard, and nearly toppled to the ground. "Do you have a damn pass, or what?"

My mind went blank at this. How could I not have known what I'd need? Foolish! I was foolish!

"You just can't cross into a camp, see," the soldier said, brushing his hand along my cheek. I drew back. "We got a war on in case you didn't notice . . . sir." He leered and winked. "Cub of a boy here, I'll bet, or, better than that . . ." He jostled my hat, and a rush of damp curls fell straight down my shoulders and back.

I faced him straight on, my hands on my hips. "I said it's an emergency. Please help me find my father." I stood my ground. My heart was racing, but I'd come too far to give up now.

"I'll see what I can do . . . miss." He strode away, chuckling some. "And if you are dying, I'm a straw-footed Rebel." I slammed my hat back on my head. "Which way to the 2$^{nd}$ New Hampshire?" I yelled after him. "Keep here," he answered, laughing hard. "Don't die on us, now." A boil of anger rose up hard in me. I'm not waiting for anyone, I swore to myself, and ran headlong toward the first pitched tent I saw. I burst into the tent, knocking hard into a half-dressed soldier just as he was holding a razor to his cheek. He wheeled around whipping shaving soap all over my face and coat. "What in Hades? I'll beat you blue!" He pushed me to the ground, his foot on my chest. At the sight of me sprawled on the floor of the tent and helpless, he emptied the rest of the shaving water all over me. He reached for his rifle. "Summoner Bradford!" I yelled loud as can be. "Summoner Bradford! He'll know me." "Sergeant!" he shouted out the tent flap. "Intruder!" The gun was pointed at me. Three men pushed into the tent. One of them was my father. The soldier, half his face shaved and looking like a striped raccoon, motioned to me. I must have looked a fright; a mass of coat, hair and mud covered boots splayed on the floor. My father knelt over me.

"My God, Maddie."        "Please, sir," the shaving soldier said, "this brat barged right in!"

"I'll take it from here," my father said.

"The 'it' is me, right, Papa?" I summoned sass, swallowing the bile in my throat.        "Do something about her, Private Bradford," a soldier ordered. "We leave soon."

"Yes, sir," my father answered, holding me tight.

When the soldiers backed out of the tent, my father picked me up in his arms.

He wiped my face with the sleeve of his coat. "My God, child, this is madness. I'm sending you straight back to my sister."        "No! No! No!" I yelled. "I'm not going back!"

My father slapped my face. He'd never struck me. We both jumped back, horrified.        "Oh, Maddie, I'm sorry, I—"        There was a thudding of booted feet outside the tent. "Private Bradford?" a voice called. "Muster, and inspection. The Captain's orders."

Just as my father lifted the tent flap, I slipped past him, dropped low, and crawled under horse's legs and shiny, new soldier boots, sliding along like an eel on a river bottom.  If my father tried to push through the masses of men and mounts to come after me, I was long gone, having shinnied up an oak tree, hidden in the thick branches.        "Maaaadddiiie!" My father's cry was muted by the stamping and snorting of the horses.

"I love you, Papa," I whispered.

I stayed up in that tree until the endless ant-line of soldiers wound their way out of the campgrounds. My body was aching, my stomach rumbling with hunger. I must have been there for at least four long hours.

A lone picket—one of the soldiers who'd caught me—paced to and fro beneath the tree. I could hear his sighs like he was breathing in my ear. I dared not move. At last he mounted his horse, spurring him to a gallop.

Now what? I looked down to see if any horses had been left behind for me to ride. There were none in sight. I swore to myself that I'd find a way to follow my father's regiment.

I shinnied down the tree trunk. Just as my feet neared the ground, someone grabbed me by the leg.

## Seven

I aimed my boot at his head. "Stop!" he yelled, "I'm—" He dodged another kick. "I'm here to help you." He tucked me up under his arm like I weighed nothing and carried me to an open rig. I twisted and kicked against him. "Let me go!" I yelled. He staggered, and then caught himself. Was I being kidnapped?

"Get in, head down," he ordered, lifting me inside the rig. My coat hung in tatters from being torn by branches. It was flapping behind me as I slumped behind him in the seat, trying to catch my breath.

I pulled my revolver out of my boot, and pointed it at him.

"Don't shoot!" He pushed back the slouch hat that nearly covered his face. I saw black, shiny curls. And eyes, well, that were greener than green. It was Jake Whitestone.

"How dare you!" I shouted.

"Dare I what? Rescue you?"

"Follow me, find me, and chase me!" I was steaming mad, and relieved that he wasn't a Rebel. Or maybe he was, and I didn't know what to think. I was really tired, and hungry and thirsty, and—

He handed me a canteen. I gulped the water.

"Find your strength," he said. Then he gave me a piece of hardtack. The cracker was rock-solid. I bit down but couldn't make a dent. *Find your strength.* He slapped the reins. "Get, now get!" The horse vaulted forward.

"Where are you taking me?"    "Your father's regiment is going to face General Beauregard at Manassas Railroad Junction. It's a twenty-mile ride," Jake Whitestone said, his back to me.    "How do you know this?"

"Centreville is two miles from Manassas," he said. "I figured it out from there."

"It's twenty-two and three-quarters miles, exactly. I know just where. I've studied a map of Virginia," I snapped, bouncing and pitching in the carriage seat.

Whatever Jake Whitestone was doing there, at least he was getting me closer to my father. I'd leave him at Centreville no matter what.

"I've never driven a rig like this, so hold on," he shouted over the crunch and crackle of wheels and reins. "And if you hit me again, I'll throw you out. I rescued you, remember?"    "Oh, yeah? I was doing just fine until you showed up."

The map in my head told me that we had to wind along New Hampshire Avenue, going straight down to reach the Potomac River and cross over at the Long Bridge. The streets were clogged with pedestrians and wagons as usual, but there weren't many soldiers among them. Had all the Union troops gone into Virginia?

I smelled a briny and swampy odor I was sure must be the river. I knew once we crossed it we would be on the Confederate side.

Two soldiers stood near a wooden hut. They raised up their rifles as our carriage drew close. One of them leaned down and took a long look at me. His rifle butt was really close to my face.

"What is your business?"

I started to speak, but Jake interrupted me. "My little brother here got drunk back in Washington City. I have to get him back to Centreville before my Pa finds out he's missing."

The soldier studied me, the ragged boy I was pretending to be.

"Yesh, sir," I slurred my voice. "I can't stand up for nothing. Jeez, all I had was a pint of ale, jeez."

"Shut up, Tommy," Jake said, producing a paper and waving it in the soldier's face. "I'm with the medical corps. After I get rid of him, I'm going on to Manassas. I hear they'll be a fight."

"Praise God, yes," the other soldier said. He looked nervous. I realized he was really young. His blue uniform looked brand new. "Go on over," he said. "Sober up that smelly kid there. Get going before I change my mind."

Jake saluted them, and we started over the bridge.

I was amazed at how Jake handled the pickets. And he called me Tommy! I couldn't help but smile to myself. But I sure wasn't going praise him to his face.

Right then, Jake ducked as a bullet sailed straight over his head and crashed into a tree. The horse reared up, nearly pitching over the carriage.    "Damn, I missed!" a voice shouted from behind us.    "Do you have a weapon?" I grabbed Jake's arm.          "No." He slapped the reins, hard.        The horse stumbled over a rock, nearly tipping us over again.    I pulled out my gun. "I know how to use this, even if you don't."

"Sure I do," he answered in a wobbling voice, turning the color of ash. Did I mention that Jake Whitestone had really pale skin?

A man with red, tangled hair, wearing a jacket striped green and yellow, galloped past, his revolver pointed straight at us.        I aimed at the man. My God, could I shoot him if I had to?

"Go, go!" Jake yelled at the horse.        The man lowered his weapon and spat into the air. "Not worth it!" the man laughed. "Itty bitty pea fowl in that buggy. I got bigger to catch. I got to kill me some Yanks!" Cursing and laughing, he sped past us.        I slumped back into the seat, my back sore, and my body weak with hunger.

"Are you okay?" I asked.

"Of course," he answered, his voice a bit shaky. "Are you?"

"Of course." I wasn't really okay at all, but darned if I was going to tell him.

43

I kept dozing off, and jerking back awake as we passed through miles of beautiful farmlands. Horses and cows grazed in the green tall grasses. Spring flowers dotted hillsides. Far back from the road sat wide-porched houses, with low-slung ramshackle buildings—shanties—scattered behind them. Negro men, women, and children, lines of them, trudged through the fields. The men were pushing plows. Even women with babies in slings were carrying heavy bags on their backs. Now and again a white man on a horse would appear wielding a whip. I saw a young Negro man down on the ground, his shirt in tatters, his back bloodied.

"Welcome to Virginia," Jake said.

I was too stunned to answer. Sure I'd seen so many different, unsettling things in Washington City, but the sights, the truth of what people did to one another made a deep furrow of pain in my heart. I will never forget these moments as long as I live.

From afar, Centreville was a town of low-lying wooden buildings, clusters of soldiers milling about, some mounted, some not. Jake Whitestone veered off the road into a grove of tall oaks. We pushed further into a glade where the air dipped to coolness, and there was nary a sound except for the bubble and rush of a stream.

"We'll camp here, and follow the regiment as soon as they move," Jake said, unhitching the horse.

"Thanks for the ride," I answered, heading away. He really muddled me. *I* was really muddled myself. But I had to get to my father. So I just ran. I was so tired and clumsy in the stupid old boots, I stumbled as I scrambled over some rocks and fallen tree limbs.

He caught up to me.

"Let me go!" I pushed him away. "Unless you want a fight."

"Go then, you damn fool! They're in camp now, not moving. If you even spot your father, he'll send you back! Is that what you want? Or are you really crazy enough to think you can pass as a soldier? "

"Yes!"

"How?"

"I don't know, yet. I'll figure it out!"

"Crazy, and dangerous, and . . . forget it." He wheeled around and limped off.

I sat down on a tree stump. Okay, I thought, what the heck do I do now? He's got the horse and buggy. I'd keep my distance from him and then make a decision. Right. I'd steal the horse.

I crept close to the buggy. No good. Jake was there, hoisting a feedbag. I'd have to wait until nightfall. "I'll feed the horse," I said.

Giving me a wary look, he handed me the feedbag. I slipped it over the animal's neck. The poor horse looked as weary as I felt. At least someone was eating.

Jake Whitestone handed me down a wrinkled, homespun dress and a heavy blanket. "Mrs. Salome's laundry pile does come in handy," he said. "Wash up, for all our sakes, and change back to your true self, I might add."

Rudely, I yanked the dress from him. He turned his back to me. "Your true self is not so bad," he said, walking away. "Call me when you're done." I think I must have turned fifty shades of red when I heard that.

I kept walking, following the sound of water on rocks. Just ahead was a stream. I stood there for a moment. Should I run off? Find my father's camp? What if he wasn't there? Oh, but the water looked so inviting, and I was so weary. I plunged my hands into the stream, and splashed my face. Coolness, blessed coolness. I lowered my head and drank like a parched animal.

My filthy clothes felt like they were plastered on me. I glanced around. No, Jake Whitestone wasn't limping through the brush. I would have heard him approaching anyway, right?

Slowly I removed the jacket. I waited, listening.

Next, the ragged pants. And oh, those killing boots! Off they went. I held the revolver over my head with one hand, and waded waist-high into the stream in just my bodice and pantaloons.

With one hand, I splashed water on my face and hair again. My curls ran with dirt into long, wet tendrils. Oh, how good it felt. My aching body slowly relaxed, my face and eyes washed clean of grit.

"If you're through, help me make camp," Jake called out.

I cleared out of that that stream in an instant, grabbed up the blanket and dried myself. I threw on the dress. With no corset at hand, and no petticoats, the dress felt soft and giving against my skin.

"Come on!" he called again.

When I returned to our camp, Jake was scooping pine needles into his hands, sitting flat on the ground, his bad leg stretched out, looking wan and tired.

"You look better clean," he said.

Without saying anything to him—and believe me, I did want to sass him good—I broke a three-forked branch off a tree and used it as a rake. In minutes I had a large, soft pile of pine needles topped with leaves. He'd be better off on something soft than lying on the ground. Oh boy, why did I care?     I backed away and motioned to the pile. He lay down on it, and sighed.

"Have you got food?" I asked. "And don't tell me just hardtack."

He was rubbing his leg as though to put strength back in it. "In the rig, in a tin box." His voice was weary. "Please, can you fetch it?"

Why didn't I answer? Why was I being so rude? Wasn't he trying to help me? You know how sometimes you get all the words ready to say and nothing comes out? Yes, that was me.

I climbed into the rig, rummaged around until I found the tin box. Inside were apples and walnuts and a bit of cheese.

Should I flee? No. Food first.

I cracked the nuts with a rock with nary a break in them, as I'd seen Mama do.

We gobbled the food.

I'd never been alone with any man other than my father, and yet I felt no fear. Strange, it was, and new and . . . okay, it was exciting.

How would I get away? And then it hit me. Did I really want to?

Jake Whitestone stared at me as though he was reading my thoughts. I knew he couldn't but it made me feel warm, jittery, and anxious, all at once.

I found a place for myself a good distance from him under a willow tree. Jake Whitestone lay down, his eyes closed.

I sat there watching him, the way his young face relaxed, the rise and fall of his chest, and—

A hawk screeched overhead. Night birds were descending. A bat flew out of a tree, seesawing into the sky. Things, live things chirred and chittered in the bushes. Late day was fading, night loomed.

While I was focusing on every little sound, I noticed Jake was awake, staring at me.

"Why don't you get some rest," he said, moving his leg and wincing from pain. I felt sorry for him right then.

"My mother would make a plaster of nettles and mustard grass, to take the ache out of that leg of yours," I said. "But I can't scout out those things with so little light."

Darkness was closing over the canopy of trees. In the distance, horses whinnied and I could hear the low voices of soldiers, the clanking of cook pots, and smell the sharp, acrid tang of fire smoke. I leaned back against the trunk of a sturdy oak, listening, ever listening for the smallest sounds of hoof beats, the calls of moving soldiers. Why were they staying put, I wondered. What were they waiting for?

Jake's voice was quiet, and very sad. "I wish I could turn back time, to stop the omnibus from crushing my leg when I was four years old. And killing my mother when she jumped out to help me."

"My mother died six months ago," I said. I felt a sharp pain where my heart was. I hadn't spoken about her until that moment.

"I'm really sorry, Miss Bradford."

He moved a bit closer to me, slowly, like he was approaching a deer that was about to bolt away. I didn't bolt, but I was ready. I'd never been in a situation anything like this before. I was uneasy and curious at the same time.

"I hardly remember my mother," he said. "We lived in Georgia. My father was a cotton merchant. He decided to move New York, where his business was headquartered. He was making piles of money off the backs of slaves. I'd seen plenty of their suffering and it never seemed right to me, but then I heard Mr. Lincoln speak at Cooper Union about how no man should ever be in chains. Oh, how I agreed! I was in school in New York and after classes, working at a job . . . well, it was something I'd always wanted to do."

"What job was that?" I asked

"It was . . . teaching, teaching children. I love children." He was rambling a bit. Maybe he was just tired. "I hardly saw my father," Jake said. "When the war started, he declared his allegiance to the Confederate cause. He said now that Lincoln was elected President, he swore he'd take me far into the south. I refused to go. He hit me hard and told me to get out. I stayed in a sad old rooming house full of poor people and women, who, well, were not seemly, and then I was sent, I mean, I came to Washington City.

"To join the fighting?" Right away I felt guilty. That was of nasty of me to say. I could see his leg was really bad. "Wait here," I said, heading for the stream. I scooped up a bit of wet mud.

I went over to Jake. "Rub this on your leg," I said stiffly.

He did just that. "It's warm, then cooling, then, oh, God, that feels better. Thank you."

His face relaxed. He moved his leg back and forth. I started away.

"Please stay," he said. "I want to tell you something."

"Okay." I have to admit, I wanted to stay.

"I'm ashamed that I cannot be a soldier," he said, closing his eyes. "I'm nearly eighteen, old enough to serve in that way." "Why did you follow me?" I asked. And what should I do, I wondered? I stood up and moved a bit closer, my hands on my hips. "Why did you follow me?" I asked again when he didn't answer. "Why?"

"I need to be here too," he said, avoiding my eyes.

"Why?"

"None of your business," he said. "Sorry, I didn't mean to be rude, Miss Bradford. I'm . . . I'm trying to help, okay?"

"I don't need your help!" My face was close to his.

"It's not holiday for me either!" He was steaming mad. So was I. Mad at myself, really. Why didn't I just leave him? When you feel things and can't say what you feel, it really is hard, isn't it?

47

"I don't need you to watch over me. Do you get that, Jake Whitestone? If anything, you're the one who needs help what with your leg, and all the rocks we've climbed and—" I backed away, feeling bad about what I'd said. "I'm sorry, it's not your fault your leg was hurt and you can't fight in this war," I said, throwing Jake Whitestone a blanket.

I guess I was staying there with him after all. Worse, I didn't mind.

To quiet the quivers in my heart, I moved even further away.     I curled up the way Papa showed me to be safe in a forest, or anywhere: my body rounded in a ball, one arm covering my head just above the eyes, the other holding the revolver.

I could hear Jake snoring lightly. Just as I nodded somewhere near a doze, I heard footfalls. Maybe an animal padding though the trees. Two footfalls, then. Closer. I gripped my gun. Tightly.                    A tall, young Negro man, a bandanna wrapped around his hair, crept along through the trees, pausing just in front of me. Something about him rang familiar. What was it? He held the hand of a woman with an infant in a carrier cloth. A small child clutched her skirts. She was dressed in a ragged skirt with a brown coat thrown over her shoulders. He had a knife in his hand.

I sat up, closing my fingers tight around the gun. He held the knife out as though to attack me then and there. I remained stock still, holding his hard gaze with my own. Just as he stepped closer, the knife outstretched, I motioned to Jake Whitestone sleeping a few yards away and put my finger to my lips. He paused. I was holding my breath. He lowered the knife, then nodded sharply and slipped by us.     I exhaled for so long, I swore the air around me moved a fraction and a startled spider jumped from a leaf to the ground.

I'd seen the man before. Or had I? I focused hard. The way he moved reminded me of the tall woman carrying the laundry basket in the alley. And the man I'd seen at the alley door? Were they one in the same?

I would tell no one what I'd seen, not even Jake. I wasn't sure if I could trust him, yet.

I slept fitfully, but for how long? When I opened my eyes it was dawn, clouded and misty. I jumped up, trying to catch a sound from the soldiers' camp. All was still.

"They've gone," said Jake.

I ran to hitch up the horse, piling the blanket and food box into the carriage. Jake came limping behind me.

"Hurry!" I yelled.

We left the forest at a gallop.

# Eight

"Follow the soldiers!" I shouted as I spotted horses streaming ahead of us, surrounded by swirls of dust.

"We're going to the ridge up ahead," Jake called out as the carriages thundered along.

"No! I have to get to my father!"

"You can't! It's too dangerous," he shouted back.

I started to climb out of the carriage. My foot caught on the spinning wheels, pitching me back against Jake. I was gasping and kicking. Jake forced the horse to a stop, knocking us both forward.

"Get out, Miss Bradford. See how far you get."

*Not far, not far. How in heck would I get anywhere? I had to stay with him.*

"I'm going to the ridge just ahead," he said. "Staying or going?"

I slumped back down in the seat.

As we rounded a bend in the road, a woman with long, blonde hair unfurled like a flag galloped toward us, going away from the direction of the soldiers, back toward Washington City, just the way we had come.       When she drew closer, I recognized her immediately as the girl called Betty Duvall, the one I'd seen in the city who'd spilled her tresses between a man's hands: the glowing, fine-featured face, scarlet cheeks, and ropes of shining hair.

Her horse was pouring sweat, and she was whipping the animal so hard that the foam flew from its mouth. She thundered along and was soon obscured by the dust kicked up by her steaming mount, swirling in circles over our heads, filling our noses and mouths.       And out of that swirl there came a sudden babble of voices as we neared a crested ridge. Bushes and trees exploded with all manner of men in dray carts: Negroes atop gleaming coaches with shiny horses at the head; gaudy, American flag-bedecked huckster women's wagons with cakes, bottles of champagne, and cooking pots rattling as they bounced along; cigar-puffing, stove-pipe wearing gents, scribbling on pads, and holding maps up high as they jostled by. Elegant ladies with sunbonnets festooned with colored ribbons, others with their slaves holding umbrellas over their heads, carried picnic baskets. It was a ridiculous, festive air, with shouts of "On to Richmond! Damn the Rebels! Death to the Union! Fresh peaches, peaches fine! Pies, and honey cakes, ginger tarts!" I heard the excited whoops of children, acting like they were about to go to the circus.

A cannon boomed loudly in the distance, like a clap of thunder swallowed mid-sound, just before the lightening hits. We moved as a bubbling mass to the edge of the ridge, swept along like minnows swirling in a pond by this broth of spectators. Finally, we found a spot on the overlook.       "Huzzah!" someone

50

shouted in a high-toned English accent. "It begins!" The shouting man jumped from his horse, pencil and pad in hand. He dropped to his knees, scribbling on the pad. He was portly and sweating in dress tweeds, with a sharp-cut black mustache in the shape of an anvil. "The time," he yelled, "what hour exactly is it now?"

"Ten in the morning, Mr. Russell, sir," a spiffed-up Negro in a linen duster called down to the kneeling man.      Jake Whitestone left the carriage, limped over, and squatted next to Mr. Russell on the ground. With a look of certain surprise, then scorn at the sight of him, though he tried to hide it, Mr. Russell said nothing, but quickly turned back to his writing pad, covering the surface with his arm. Did they know each other?      With like force, two more men, their paper pads and pencils clutched in their teeth, landed like pelicans, nearly atop one another. "Make way for the *Charleston Courier*," a small man dressed in black brayed like a donkey.      "Sure, Rebel," another said. "I'll write to the world of your defeat."      Another resounding *boom!* A deep voice rose over the excited babble. "Our yanks have got Parrott rifles, bless them cannons!"      "They're green and raw, those boys, but they bloody well shall not die without my tribute," Russell said. He pointed to an elaborate carriage making its way through the crowd. "It's the British delegation, come to witness," he crowed. "Huzzah! Make way!" "They're British diplomats, judges, congressmen, and senators," a woman shouted.

They were slapping each other on the back, with cries of "Bravo!" and "Isn't this fine?"      A chicken leg landed square on the *Charleston Courier* reporter's head. He jumped to his feet and punched wildly, hitting a woman right in the mouth as she balanced two pies in her hands. Berries and dough splattered everywhere.      Jake Whitestone lay on his stomach peering through his field glasses. I dropped down next to him and tried to see. All below was a tree-shrouded blur, save for a distant roadway beyond a small ridge.      More cannons rumbled.

I whispered, "Go to the Warrenton Turnpike. I see it in the distance. We can get closer." *And then I'll find my papa*, I thought. *My God, I hope he is all right.*

"How do you know these things? You've never been here!" He looked at me as though I'd dropped down from the sky.

I didn't tell him about my fine-tuned memory. Why should I? Don't you agree?      Jake Whitestone pulled me to my feet. We pushed our way to the carriage and were off, back down the overlook, nearly running over more celebrating women holding children, dragging wagons of hams, tin buckets piled with bread loaves, and more bottles of wine and sarsaparilla.      *"Rebels dancing at the end of a noose, bobbing like apples, fast and loose,"* someone sang.      Once we crossed the road out of Centreville toward the turnpike, it seemed we had lost most of the spectators who'd settled in for their Sunday picnic. I imagined them now sprawled, full of food, on the ridge, pitching marbles and chicken bones down into the trees.

51

*F*inally we came to a point overlooking a stone bridge with a running stream about a mile away. Puffs of smoke and artillery fire echoed loudly. Was my father down there? Hurt? Dying? I was beyond worried for him.

We were no longer alone. Clustered about, with mouths agape, were gentlemen in stovepipe hats.    Jake pulled up alongside them. "What have you seen?" he asked. I waited for their reply, my heart in my throat.   "They rage! Our boys will triumph, you see?" one man said. "Down there are the Union brigades, crushing the Rebels like locusts."    Jake pulled out a pair of field glasses. I grabbed them away.  For several hours we watched a massive tangle of men and weapons, impossible to tell one from the other. Sometimes they crashed together, exploding in fire and smoke. Then a sprawling line of others raced into the fray. I could hear the cries of the soldiers and the ungodly screams of horses. My own cry of "Papa!" melted into the air. Jake Whitestone tumbled and almost fell. I grabbed hold of his hand to steady him.

"A soldier in the know just passed this way," a man said. "He reports victory is ours, surely. The Rebels have fallen back into the trees, chased hard by General McDowell's diversion troops, against Beauregard's left flank. Just there below!"

"Yep!" said another man. "If the Rebs don't reinforce, the day is ours. God bless the boys of the 79th New York, the 2nd New Hampshire, and the 22nd Massachusetts!"    The Englishman Russell, full of starch and strut, appeared again. This time he raced to the edge of the ridge like a charging bull. He must have followed us. "Bully day is saved!" he crowed. "Heard that Rebels and Yanks, all of them unused to being enemies, are swarming each other like bees."

Then he jumped back into his carriage that was filled with reporters. "Washington City will be in celebration, no need to fear," one of them shouted. "On to telegraph the world!"    "It's over?" I asked, praying it was over.

"Maybe," said Jake.      "I want to go back to the city, to wait for my father. I know he'll find me," I said, willing myself to believe it. "Are you coming?" I grabbed his jacket. "No!" He said, his face set. "I *have* to stay." "I'm going now!"

"Then go!" Jake shot back, "and see how far you get."    "Love the killing? Or fear the victory? Which side are you on, Jake Whitestone?" He let go of me then and I fled through the crowd.

I looked around to see if I could hitch a ride on one of the carts and carriages that pitched and groaned all around me. I grabbed hold of the sideboard of an old cart driven by Negroes. It was piled with rakes, pitchforks and bales of hay. I threw myself in.

As it rumbled and teetered down the hill, I spotted Jake Whitestone limping toward two Confederate soldiers, their horses lathered, nearly falling. What was he doing with those Rebels? Jake Whitestone held out a hand to one of them, shook it, and walked up to a small tent. The entrance was jammed with men in civilian clothes scribbling on pads of paper. And Jake Whitestone was smiling.

## Nine

I'd landed in the cart on a pile of blankets, nearly squashing a small boy burrowed underneath them. He yelped in surprise, his eyes wide at the sight of me. A young man freed the child, all the while aiming a pitchfork at me.

"Please! I mean no harm," I shouted.

"Dropped on my boy like that? Git out this wagon!" The pitchfork was moving closer to my face.

"Let her be, Johnny," an old man said. He was missing an arm, a sleeve tucked and sewn over the empty place. "Poor ragged thing, what ken she do to us?"

The little boy piped up. "I ain't hurt, Pa. She don't have much weight on her."

"I need to get back to Washington City, to . . . to my house, to find my father. He's a Yankee." I shouted out over the din of voices, cries of horses, and the noise of wagon wheels, whistles, and yells.

The man lowered his pitchfork. "You got any money?"

"No, sir. Not a penny," I said, bouncing in the cart.

"Like as not, she be a beggar," the old man said. "If she gets out the wagon now, she could be trampled down."

The younger man's answer, or lack of one, was swallowed up again by the shouts and curses of soldiers, and the whinnying of rider-less horses careening along.

"Hang on, now," he yelled. "Hang on." We plunged through a growing crowd, a teeming mass headed away from the battlefield in the direction of Washington City.

We crossed back over the Potomac River. This time the crowds swept past the guards. They didn't give chase. There were too many coming, too fast.

I hung on to the top of the wagon rail for dear life, scanning the faces of the wounded, the walking, and the riding. Broken soldiers were carried on doors, planks of wood, anything that would act as a litter. Bandaged heads, bloody arms and legs, and the screaming of men in agony made me weak. Was my father among them? Was he even alive?

I looked for anyone in his regiment. Their uniforms were so distinctive, remember? Spike-tail coats, red cords, or hats that had "2$^{nd}$ NH" written on them. I didn't see a single soldier that looked familiar. The cart rattled on.

As we neared the city, with the road growing more impassable, the cart stopped short in front of an empty overturned wagon with two dead horses splayed across our path. Women and children ran right past, some shrieking in horror, some laughing. A child's rubber ball flew in the air. A bullet pierced it. It exploded, falling to the ground.

The young man jumped out of the cart. "Got to git this here rig out the way, Pa," he shouted. I jumped down too, and pushed hard at the wagon, as we were both trying to right it. It didn't budge.

"Best go, girl," the older man said. "Go find your pa in all this devilish mess."

"Thank you!" I clasped his hand.

From where we stopped, I could see the President's House with all manner of people clamoring at the gates. I wasn't far from the boardinghouse. I knew where to go but my head was swimming from the sounds of gunshots, screaming, and the sight of bumping, thrashing men and horses blocking my way. Blocking anyone's way. I remember that moment as a time of such madness. I felt like the little, broken kid I used to be when every noise was an assault on my ears and eyes. I stumbled to a lamppost and hung on, the roaring in my head louder than any steam engine. It felt like the world was on fire and if I burned up on the spot, no one would notice or care.

I was growing weaker. I stumbled along, weaving and bobbing like a ship in a hurricane. I had to keep stopping to catch my breath. Was this what being in battle felt like? How could anyone endure it?

I felt ashamed. Here I was, safe for the moment, and hardly a soldier at all. Find your strength, I told myself, and square up.

Just then, a wounded soldier plowed right into me, his face running with tears, his bandaged arm covered with blood.

"God, Jesus, little girl, help me!" he cried. "Water! I need water!"

I reached for his other arm and together we managed to take a few steps into the street, swept along by the crowd like fish in a raging current.

"I got a kid like you," he mumbled. "Jenny, my little Jenny, I got to see her."

*Jenny. Jenny. Jenny. Mama.* I was feeling delirious. It was hot, so hot, and— I spotted a horse trough. Men and women were lapping up water like animals. I held fast to the soldier. I pushed my way to the trough, cupped my hand in the water and held it to his mouth, then to my own. The water was dirty and warm, but oh, it tasted blessedly good. The soldier kissed my hands.

"Bless you, girl. Thank goodness, I see my captain yonder." He pointed to a group of men just beyond the water trough.

"I'm good now, Jenny," he said, moving, stumbling away.

*I'm not good, Jenny, I thought, but I'm safe for now, and by God, I'm going to find our man.*

I made it to my aunt's place more dead than alive.

## Ten

I stumbled up to the cellar door. It was unlocked. I pushed it open and tripped, falling to the floor. I was trying to get up when someone grabbed my arm and pulled me to my feet. Though there was only a single candle burning by the washbasin, I made out his face. It was the Negro man I'd seen when I was in the woods with Jake Whitestone.

He pressed a knife to my throat. "I'll cut you where you stand," he whispered.

"I'm—" I drew a deep breath, hard to do as he held me fast. My words were sputters. I took a chance and said, "I'm a friend to your mother."

There was a silence. His knife pressed harder against my throat.

"Yeah?" His breath was hot in my ear.

"What do you know about it?" He pushed me to the floor. Close by I could hear a child whimper and a woman hushing it.     "I know you are helping these people. I saw you near Centreville," I said. "In the forest. Do you remember?"

I could feel his body relax just a bit.     "I swear here and now, I will say that I didn't see you here or there, or ever," I said. As he hadn't yet killed me, I kept talking. "I'm a stranger here. Where I come from, we don't have their ways."

He drew the knife away. I moved away from him, and he grabbed me again.

"What ways?" he whispered. "Make me believe you or I'll slit your throat like a set-down hog."     "Here, they treat your kind like animals. That is a mortal sin. My father is fighting for Mr. Lincoln, all the way from New Hampshire. God's truth." I struggled to rise. With me in tow, and still holding the knife, he went to the corner of the room. "Stay low," he said to the woman I knew was there. "It's all right."     I could hear her exhale. The child began to whimper again.

"Isaac, go get them out of here, please," I said.

"You don't know my name. And don't you say nothing to my mother."

"I swear I won't."

"You best pray you speak truth," he said. "I ain't blind. I know your face." He pushed me to the floor. "Don't be moving, and shut your eyes tight." I could feel his hand on my back.

In a far part of my brain, I knew they were leaving. There were footsteps, whispers and again the whimpering of a child. I heard a low whistle, and horses chuffing and the sound of a wagon stopping just outside the door.

I lay there. There was silence. Were they gone? I let my breath out easy and struggled to my feet. My neck burned where his knife had scraped it.

Without looking back, I lurched over to the narrow staircase that led up from the cellar, and into the kitchen, I heard voices from above. I was gasping for breath. I could feel wetness on my neck.     When I reached the top of the stairs, wobbling and dizzy, I went toward the voices in the dining room. I heard the clinking of glasses and cries of *Victory! Down with the Yankees!* I fell forward in a swoon, right over a chair, and landed limp as a rag on the floor. I was conscious, but so very weak . . . from hunger, and worry, from everything. Faces swam before my eyes. I smelled roasted meat, and of all things, my head was in a puddle of Aunt Salome's s prized brandy that had spilled from the decanter, as I must have knocked the table before I fell. I tried to get up but the brandy fumes made me even dizzier.

Mr. Webster bent over me. "She breathes slightly, and there's some blood."

"My Lord, is it Madeline?" my Aunt Salome said. "I thought she'd gone missing for good!"     It was Nellie who lifted me in her arms, crooning and pressing her ear to my heart. I was fully conscious by now, but I decided to stay limp until I could figure some things out.     "She ain't dead, praise God," Nellie said. She carried me into the parlor and was about to lower me to the sofa, the special, never-to-be-soiled one my aunt guarded like it was made of diamonds.

"Not there!" my aunt called. "Take her to the cellar and wash her off in the privy."

*No!* I thought. Nellie's son and the slaves might still be there.

I sat straight up, startling them. "No! My room, I need my bed!"     Nellie carried me up the stairs while the rest remained below, muttering to each other.

In my room, spare as it was, the bed was blessedly soft. "Oh, child," Nellie said, wiping my face with a damp cloth, "What done become of you?"

"My father? Has he come here?"     "No, baby, there's been soldiers and their wounded in the streets for hours. He ain't come . . . yet."     "Were Aunt Salome and Mr. Webster celebrating?" I asked in a voice much stronger than I felt.

"Hush, child."

"Were they?" I grasped her hands.

"Yes, they was cheering the Yankee defeat, talking about how them soldiers was running back to the city like rats, I'm afeered," Nellie answered, her face grave.     "Oh, Nellie." I pressed myself to her bosom, tears running from my eyes. "There, now, there now," was all she said. "I'm going to fetch the hip bath and some hot water. I got to see you ain't broke anywhere under all this here dirt."

"Wait, Nellie." I grabbed her hand again. "I know about your son."

She drew away from me.

"He's helping slaves escape, isn't he?"

"You don't know nothing, Miss Madeline, you hear?"     "I came upon them, or they came upon me, uh, him, I was in the woods, and I saw him, or someone exactly like him guiding a woman and child through the trees."

Nellie put her hands over her face.

"He's gone, Nellie. But he was just in the cellar with the same people.

Nellie's hands trembled. "Oh, Lord."

"I'll never tell anyone, Nellie. I swear it."     Nellie was shaking all over. "That's why you wanted your bed, and not the cellar like Mrs. Salome ordered me?" "Yes," I answered.

Her voice was ragged with emotion. "My son Isaac, he is my heart. And he tears at it until it has gone to fraying with fear."     "He's brave, Nellie." I leaned my head back, accidentally exposing the knife scratch on my neck.     "He hurt you!" she cried.     "No. Some. It doesn't matter." "Yes, it does." With that, she handed me a clean, white cloth. "Hold this 'crost your neck, baby. I'll come back."

I passed out the minute she left the room.     When I woke, through waves of dizziness, I saw a figure sitting by the bed, watching me. I couldn't make out just who it was because it was like I was seeing though a glass in blinding sunlight.

"Papa?" I reached toward the figure. A hand clasped mine. It was warm and strong.

For a moment, I was small again, and hugging his shoulders as we waltzed in the meadow, just near the river.

"They say you are all right, Miss Madeline."

His face was not yet in focus.     I blinked again and again.

"You made it back in one piece," he said. "I figured you would. You're a real scrapper."

I blinked hard. His face was blurred. I blinked again. Papa? No. Kind green eyes and black hair, curling black hair, hands holding mine.

"Miss Madeline, oh, Miss Madeline," Jake Whitestone said, sighing.

I felt so many things just then. Feelings like pebbles pelted me. Relief, a kind of joy at seeing Jake, worry for my father, and disappointment it wasn't him.

I tried to get up. I was so weak that when I stood I fell forward. He caught me in his arms. I was frozen for a moment. His face was so close to mine, he held me tightly. His hair brushed my cheek.

I pushed him away, trying to catch my breath. "I have to find my father!"

I tottered past him to the door. Mr. Webster, my aunt and Nellie were blocking the entrance.

"Get out of my way!

My aunt took my arm. "Get back to bed, Madeline. Right now," she said.

"No! I have to get out of here!"

They surrounded me. There was no escaping them. Mr. Webster was looking tenderly at me. But who was he, really? I'd seen him in front of the Greenhow house in disguise!

And Jake Whitestone, well, I didn't know what he was feeling. Did I care? Yes! No, maybe. I didn't even know what side he was on. Or my aunt, for that matter. And Nellie, with her fierce son Isaac putting himself and his mother in great danger? Had he left the house? And my father, where was he?

You might be thinking right now that maybe I started screaming. You'd be wrong.

I sat back down on the bed. I'll get away from them, somehow, I thought.

"Okay, I'll rest. Just leave me alone." I lay back with my eyes closed. I had to make a plan.

I heard shouting from the street. "Yankee cowards!"

My God.

"The Rebs won the day!" My heart nearly stopped.

But how had they won? What had happened? I sure wasn't going to ask my aunt, or Mr. Webster, or—

Jake Whitestone walked to the bed.

"Stay away!"

I felt like slapping him hard. I reached out to do just that. I figured he was a shifty rebel. He stopped my hand and held it to his chest. I pried it away.

"After you ran off, I was on the battlefield, Miss Madeline."

"Darn right you were, glad-handing a bunch of Rebels."

"Yes I was."

"Whose side are you on, Jake Whitestone?"

"How can you ask me that?"

"I saw you!"

"Yes, I was with soldiers and reporters—it's my job!"

"Your job? Liar! You said you were a tutor."

"No, I'm not." He spoke in a monotone. "Sixty men of the 2$^{nd}$ New Hampshire got captured by the Confederates, Miss Madeline," he said. "Seven were killed. I wish I could tell you more." His face was full of pain. "Dead boys lay so thick. My God." He grasped my hand again, so hard my fingers were going to numbness.

"Word is that Rebel intelligence reached Beauregard," he said, "reporting our positions, urging reinforcements from Johnston. The rebels were warned, but how?"

I remembered what I'd seen in the alley. Could it be Betty and Colonel Jordan brought news of the Union position to the Rebels?

Her masses of hair and the message it held. I just knew it, I—

Jake Whitestone gasped. The cloth had slipped from my neck. "What happened to you?" "Wire, wire on a fence, that's all." He touched the thin line of red, no longer bleeding, a zig-zagging, tiny line.

"I'm okay." I pulled away. His touch sent shivers though me. "I'm okay. It's just a scratch."

61

He held some sheets of paper full of writing in his hand. "This dispatch is in today's paper," he said. "I figured you should see it. As soon as I go back, I'll telegraph another one. I have to find out what happened, and why we got so badly defeated."

He touched my face, gently, so gently.

"I'm a reporter, not a tutor, Miss Madeline. Mr. Horace Greely gave me a chance to write for him, even though they'd never hired anyone so young. I begged him," he said, handed me the sheet of paper. "You asked what I was doing here? Well, I have a war to fight too."

Without saying another word, he left my room.

When I read this, I was stunned, angry, and, well, with all that had happened, just plain mixed up. Jake was Pan, and he'd written about me. The fierce little creature he spoke of had to be me. I wasn't dreaming! We were together from the time he pulled me down from the tree. He used me! Or did he? What do you think?

### *New York Tribune*

**Special from Washington CityI was heading for the battle, and along the way, I found her, or should I say rescued her. Or maybe she rescued me. Of what stuff was she made, this fierce little creature that raged at me? My bruises from the encounter notwithstanding, the being had a mighty strength, not to mention the hard right hook of a prized pugilist.**

**But oh, she is brave.     Is this yet another face of this just war? The civilian little she-scrappers who wanted in on the fight? Does this hellion speak, or should I say, shout for us all?     What is their duty? What is mine?   No time to tarry, reader. I'm going back.        PAN**

I threw the paper across the room, fuming, and fascinated, and to be honest, really, really sorry to see Jake go.

Nellie came into the room carrying a bucket of steaming water. She closed the bedroom door. "The cellar is clean now. I saw to it myself," she said, her eyes piercing into mine. I breathed a heavy sigh of relief.     Nellie was mute as she soaped me with the blessedly warm water. Finally, she spoke. "My boy ain't no threat to you now. You understand?"   "I understand that Isaac is brave," I said.

"Them folks he gets to freedom? If the slave catchers find him, they'll kill him and send the others back to be punished bad." She knelt by the bath and prayed. Then, she wrapped me in a blanket and helped me to my bed.

The last thing I imagined I saw before sleep overtook me - you know that dozy, dreamy state where you are conscious but not really - I thought I saw my father. He was surrounded by a bunch of cheering, Rebel soldiers. My father was kneeling on the ground, his head down, his rifle smashed to pieces. I was gasping.

My head was whirling. I got straight out of bed and paced the floor the rest of the night.

*

The next morning, before I dragged myself down to breakfast, I found this paper slipped under my door. It was folded to the page you'll read now.

**Special Dispatch from the *New York Tribune***

At first the Union retreat was orderly, a withdrawal, they called it. Those who cried victory to Mr. Lincoln's soldiers, the overzealous, frothing reporters, were dead wrong. By some means or Rebel miracle, word was gotten to Generals Johnston and Beauregard. They crested Henry Hill just near the stone bridge over Bull Run after learning that Rebel reinforcements were desperately needed—the right place at just the right moment.     But how were they summoned? There was no time, unless someone had gotten a dispatch through Confederate lines.     And yet, they came, a steady, ready stream of Rebel fighting men. Like lions they devoured the Union troops, sending them flooding the roads and farms, routing them in a wild skedaddle all the way back to Washington City.     Earlier dispatches, some from the great pen of the mighty, much-celebrated English reporter Russell, got it dead wrong.     This reporter was no fortune-teller, readers, he just waited atop a perch overlooking the fighting as the last of the partygoers, politicos, pie-hawkers, and war-watchers trickled away. And he saw the flight, saw the jumble of untried soldiers, some leaving their dead where they lay, scrambling back to their camps.     The roads were clogged with these same revelers who'd heard of an early victory, now stunned at the sight of the bodies of the dead and wounded strewn amid the remains of blackberry pies and liquor bottles, nearly trampled by young warriors screaming for their mothers, damning their generals, and tumbling down hillsides making masses of dust that clogged the eyes and ears.     And where was the little scrapper, a girl who'd been a strange comfort to this lumbering reporter? I thought long and hard of her as I watched her leave the chaos.     "My father is down there," she cried. "My father." May she find safety. May he as well.     This is official, no matter what you've read. Mr. Lincoln's army has suffered a great defeat. Humiliation is in the air, reader, as is fear of a Rebel invasion. What will become of Washington City now?     I am going to get a sense of what is to come, reader, to mingle, as they say, with both sides. Might reporters from Mr. Greeley's paper be endangered because we are so firm in our stand for Mr. Lincoln, unlike Mr. Bennett's Herald, which seems to appease and flatter? Perhaps. It matters not to this faithful scribe. Onward.     PAN

If Jake Whitestone could get information, so could I. You might think that was foolish. What could I do, a girl alone in the city? Well, I vowed to find a way. After all, I remembered so many details, heard so many things. I knew what I'd seen in that alleyway, and saw the girl called Betty riding away. And Mr. Webster's disguise had to mean something. I decided to find him, if he was still at the boardinghouse.

In all the long, sad, months of Mama's sickness, I feared the passing of time. Not anymore.

## Eleven

Just after breakfast, Mr. Webster came into the parlor. I cornered him as he was heading up the stairs.

"Sir, Mr. Webster, I must speak with you in private."        "You're looking in the pink, Miss, and glad we all are of it," he said. "Or should I say, in the red. Are you fevered?"        I spoke softly.        "Are you a Pinkerton man?"

He paused; his expression hardened, and then replied calmly. "I am as I appear to be."

"A Rebel and a slaver?" I asked. I studied his face, waiting for him to say more.

"Oh, now Miss," he said, "don't tell me you worry over the poor cotton pickers whose labors fill the coffers of both sides of this . . . struggle," he said, patting my hand, a condescending smile on his face. He tried to pass me to go upstairs.        I blocked his way again. "No, sir. That is not it at all. Hear me, please, sir." I took a deep breath. "I saw you at Mrs. Greenhow's house."

He blinked twice, but did not speak.

"You were dressed as a clergyman."

His eyes bored into mine.

"I am not mistaken, sir," I said slowly.

"I have no idea what you are talking about, Miss Bradford." He brushed past me. "A clergyman, indeed."

"Mr. Webster. I know I am very young, but I have certain . . . abilities. I know what I saw."

He exhaled, all the while studying my face. Finally, Mr. Webster took my hand. "The day promises to be not so stifling, warm and bright," he said, his tone measured. "I'll show you a bit of the city. We'll speak further. Yes?"

I hesitated. Should I go anywhere with this man? Would you have gone anywhere with this man?

But the chance to get away from the boardinghouse, and my aunt, was very, very tempting. I felt like a prisoner there, especially since I'd run away to find my father's camp, and Aunt Salome was watching me like a hawk.

"Yes, sir, I think I would like to go."

"Be ready in two hours." Mr. Webster turned on his heel, and left the room.

"Madeline! Where have you gotten to?" Aunt Salome called.

I was right near her. She didn't have to yell out. Even when she spoke softly, and she rarely did, it was impossible not to hear her, as her voice was like metal scraping against metal. I could hardly wait for Mr. Webster to summon me. I was excited, and nervous, but mostly excited.

"I'll be right there, Aunt."

I followed her up the stairs, glancing at the carved ebony grandfather clock that chimed hourly: a deep pealing, like a mourning bell, or an announcement of something important.

Two hours, Mr. Webster said.

I felt a bit uneasy going off with a man who surely was not what he seemed. But I sensed I'd called his bluff. If he was on the right side, and Aunt Salome was clearly not, what was I doing here, and how could I help? If he wasn't, and I'm not being dramatic, he could kill me. But deep inside, I really sensed he was not my enemy. I decided to trust that feeling.

As I sorted the boarders' clean laundry that poor Nellie had hauled to their rooms, and as Aunt Salome arranged them in a basket, I sat straight down on a pile of newly washed shirts. On purpose.

"Madeline! Get up, they'll wrinkle!"

I did not move. "When I fainted and broke your brandy decanter," I asked, "was there some sort of celebration happening?"    Aunt Salome's mouth drew up tight. "Stand up right now. Madeline, you are crushing Mr. Webster's fresh shirts." She grasped my wrist.    "Do you rejoice for the Rebels, Aunt, while my father risks his life for a cause just and true?"    "Impudence," she said loudly. "I don't have to explain a thing to you, dropped on me here like a one-winged hatchling." She pulled me into an empty room.    Aunt Salome closed the door and motioned to the bed. "Sit, Madeline."    "Yes, ma'am."

She had a look about her I'd never seen before: pained, angry, and intense. "Do you have any idea what it was like on my Maryland farm, after my husband burst his gut and died? Of course you don't."    "No, Aunt Salome. My father rarely spoke of your troubles," I answered, knowing his and Mama's disapproval of his sister and her husband's keeping slaves.    The words poured from her. "My husband gave me no children, not a one to warm my heart or mourn my passing. And my slaves scattered like chickens in a lightning storm, though I cared for them as my own. The tobacco plants died before they could be dried, and, I am ashamed to say, my neighbors brought me food so I would not go hungry."

She wiped away tears, flicked at them like mosquitoes.

"I care for my brother. I do not have to love his beliefs or his cause. I will rent rooms to Yankees or Confederates, as long as they pay, do you understand? But maybe with this recent Yankee defeat, both sides will turn tail and stop. And if that happens, you and your father can go home, in one piece, and I can be relieved of the responsibility of caring for you, feeding you, and oh, God, I don't know anything else but a farming life. Just like you don't know anything else, growing up with abolitionists feeding thoughts of freedom like porridge to anyone who will listen. Do you understand the risk in that?"

67

"Yes, I truly do, Aunt Salome." I remembered Mr. Amos Jefferson and how my parents had sheltered him. If we lived in the south, what might mama and papa have suffered as a result of their good deed?

My aunt was weeping. I felt pity, or at least a whisper of it, for her. Things were so much more complicated than I could ever have imagined.

"I'm sorry for your woes, Aunt Salome," I said, and I was.        "I'm not the enemy, Madeline," she said wearily, "just a tired old woman. Do you understand? Of course you do."        "Yes, ma'am," I answered, patting her hand. I'd not noticed how dry and chafed the flesh of it was, and how she was a bit bent over when she walked. "I'll manage the clothing, Aunt Salome, perhaps you should rest. And then I'm going out for a bit. Mr. Webster has offered me a stroll, a city tour, I believe he said."        "That's nice," she said, looking past me. "A fine gentleman, he is, and he pays right on time." "Aunt Salome?" "Yes?"        "I'm sorry to have burdened you," I said, meaning my words; yet knowing, hoping I was about to alter myself in ways I barely understood, but welcomed like a new morning.    "Have you seen Mr. Whitestone about?" she asked. "He's two days late with his board money."        I grabbed up a pile of shirts, until they nearly covered my face. "No, I've not," I said. My heart was in my toes at the very mention of his name.

Twelve

Mr. Webster was waiting for me as I came down the stairs. Even though I couldn't wait to go, I was seized with a moment of hesitation. He offered me his arm.

"You are safe with me, Miss Bradford. Do you understand? You are safe with me." He measured each of those words carefully. The cotton planter, the flowery, studied, frivolous manner he had, disappeared in that instant. Even his southern drawl lessened.

"Tell me more about your abilities, Miss Bradford."

Whoa, I sure wasn't going to tell him about my accident, and how hard it had been for Mama and Papa when they thought I was not right in the head.

I studied Mr. Webster. "Your right foot is larger than your left, sir. You lead with it when you walk. When you take up a knife or fork, your left pinky remains in the air, and cannot move with the rest of your fingers. But there are no scars on your hands so the injury must have occurred a long time ago."

I paused to catch my breath. Mr. Webster was regarding me intently.

"My finger has been this way since birth," he said softly. "I have to buy two different sizes of shoes. Very good, miss, very good indeed."

"You have kind eyes, sir. Yet you narrow them as though to fix your face and harden it. Your expression, your whole being changes at will."

We had reached the corner of 16$^{th}$ Street. I was so engrossed in our conversation I'd barely heard the clatter of carriages, the voices of men, wide-skirted women and scampering children.

"What else?" he asked.

"I saw you dressed as a clergyman, sir. Who are you, really?"

"You will see, Miss Bradford," he answered. He spoke with a different accent. Crisp, with no elongated vowels. A changed man stood before me. All gentlemanly courtesy was gone. His face was set, grim, hardened.

"What more did you see at Mrs. Greenhow's house? You must tell me, now," Mr. Webster said as soon as we reached the street. "Now! It is important."

I took a deep breath. Do you know how you decide to trust someone? Do you really know? Even though some uneasiness lingered, I decided to trust him, and I've never regretted it.

"Behind her house, in the alley, sir," I said, "There was . . . an exchange."

"Of what?" He grasped my arm tightly. I hesitated. "It could be very important," he said, not letting go of me.

I'd never felt important, or that things I saw meant much at all. I was elated.

"You say Mrs. Greenhow is dangerous?" I asked, remembering what the soldiers said about her.

"Lethal," he answered. "A good number of Rebels like her sit in the Old Capitol Prison as we speak. Somehow she is in direct communication with Confederates in the field. But it was not known how Mrs. Greenhow was communicating."

I took a deep breath.

"I know the face and name of her courier, I remember every detail including the name of the man she met in the alley."

"Can you identify them?"      I was silent. Should I tell him what I'd seen? I was wavering.

"Can you?" he demanded.

I waited. *If Mr. Webster was truly a Pinkerton man —*

"I want to meet him."      "Who?"      "Mr. Alan Pinkerton."

Mr. Webster stopped short. He looked me straight in the eye. "I dare say. Why?"

"I heard he helped to save President Lincoln from assassination in Baltimore when he came to Washington City to be inaugurated. I heard it on the train coming here and it was in the papers. He, all his people, must be very brave."

Mr. Webster was silent for a long time. As we walked the city streets teemed with carriages, milk wagons with bottles teetering and toppling into the mud and debris splattered on cobblestones. I lifted my skirts as a barrel rolled at me, its split sides pouring liquid, something that smelled like liquor. The fumes clogged my nostrils, and my blood raced with the din and stench of it all.

I was growing a bit dizzy, and stumbled. Mr. Webster caught my arm.

He pulled me to a lamppost, and wiped my face with his handkerchief.

"What place have you come to, little Miss, with a mind like a photographer's camera? What good fortune came my way that I found you? And what perils might you endure in my keep?"

I was speechless. No one had ever spoken to me this way. Here was a man, nearly a stranger, who valued what I was telling him, respected what I was saying and seeing and remembering. *There goes the 'village peculiar', they would say back in Portsmouth. Maybe, just maybe, now, she was shedding that old skin for another.*

I decided then and there to ask Mr. Webster what I wanted. I took the chance.

"Please, sir, my father is risking his life for what he believes. Might I not help as well in some small way?"

Mr. Webster led me to a nearby bench. He motioned for me to sit.

"Mr. Pinkerton was working as the head of a detective agency in Chicago when Samuel Felton, the President of the Baltimore and Ohio Railroad, asked him to investigate a plot against Abraham Lincoln. He came to Washington City and then sent operatives to Maryland, to unmask the conspiracy."

"And they did, right?"

"Yes," said Mr. Webster. "But there are many, many others who would like to see President Lincoln dead, the Union destroyed and this city given over to the enemy. Rebels who sneak like sewer rats."

"I want to help, sir. I know I can."

His gaze was so grave, so very grave.

"You are not ready, miss."

My heart sank. "Good day, sir." I turned back to the house, walking fast.

He didn't let me get far, but grasped my shoulder.

"You really must see a perfect representation of a great Apache warrior at the Smithsonian Picture Gallery, Miss Bradford. Have you been there?" He didn't wait for an answer but turned me away from the house. "The Apache's fierceness reaches from the canvas, and the colors are, well, astonishing," he said, stopping me in my tracks, not by a firm hand on my arm again, but by his eyes, grey and hard as marbles. "Come with me, Miss Bradford. It will be a worthy excursion for us both, mark my words."      He was moving me along the street now, past a makeshift hospital, where a group of bandaged, pale soldiers lay on a shaded veranda, through the bustle and snap of bright-faced strollers, pausing now and again to sigh with pity at a battered soldier being borne on a litter, or peering at a line of haggard Confederate prisoners dragging along between two guards holding bayonets at their backs. As we passed a beggar man, Mr. Webster patted him three times on the arm, and dropped five pennies in his wooden bucket. The man bowed, grabbed up his things, and walked quickly away.      Mr. Webster cast a sharp glance behind us, and back to me again.

"The beggar we passed just now, sir," I said, "he had the smooth, white hands of a gentleman who'd not labored, ever. He had fifteen pennies in his bucket, not counting your five."

"I dare say," he said, shaking his head with amazement, "I do dare say."

"And sometimes, if I concentrate hard, I can hear bits of conversations that others cannot," I added.

"Impressive," Mr. Webster said. "And enchanting."

I bristled at the word "enchanting." If he only knew how my strangeness used to pain me. Finally, would it, would I, be good for something?

We passed through a daisy-filled meadow. Boys and men were hollering, and laughing, shooting at cloth targets mounted on posts. "Watch your way," Webster said. "This area is a shooting range. They do miss the mark now and again." I ducked away in a flash as one bullet sailed over my head. "Very good," he said. "Quick as a penny-whistle."      In the middle of the carpet of flowers was a rust-colored castle. "That's the Smithsonian Museum," Mr. Webster said. "A marvel, eh?"

It was a bit vulgar, like huge, overdone, decorated cake, with carved spires, arched doorways, and a huge, turreted column that looked ready to pierce the clouds.      Inside, Mr. Webster whisked me past rows of white marble busts—heads of kings, Roman gods, and emperors all in neat arrangement—straight to the picture gallery, a grand hall with mahogany carvings and paintings as far as the eye could see: oils and watercolors, dazzling, costumed men and their wives, looking the lesser in their schoolmarm's lace. Beyond were soaring landscapes of the Western frontier: unforgiving, scorched plains crawling with buffalo, and Indian portraits all about, some in fancy white man's clothing, others in blazing war-paint.

I'd never been any place like this place where all time was stopped, cool-aired and very still, except for some heavy skirted women and their gentlemen escorts moving like chess pieces along the rows, now and again pausing to stop before a painting, exclaiming, criticizing, admiring in murmurs as though they were in a church. The war is invisible here, I thought.      Before I could pause to take it all in, Webster swept me to yet another large oil painting to the side of the gallery.

Across the broad canvas, Indian braves rode in silence, scouting, watching in all directions, for what? Even the horse was vigilant, looking away, perhaps an impending attack? And the colors—      Within minutes, Webster grabbed my arm and walked me hurriedly through the gallery and out the door. I blinked hard in the sunlight, my mind a jumble of images.      "Don't speak, Miss," he said. "Just remember." We passed through the daisy meadow and left the spires of the fantasy castle behind.

"What now, Mr. Webster?" I asked, sensing this excursion was a kind of test.

"I'm taking you back to your aunt, for now. Be patient."

Patient? Back to that solitude, the endless chores, for how long? I thought as Mr. Webster bid me farewell at the boardinghouse door.

            *      Two long days passed without any sign of Mr. Webster, or any word from my father. The papers had the lists of the missing and the dead in Papa's regiment. His name was not among them. But where was he?

Late in the afternoon of the second day, I was resting after my chores. To keep my mind busy, I kept going over the Indian painting in my mind. I could almost taste the dust, and feel the sweat of the Indian horses, their bodies slick with it. I remembered all I had seen in that remarkable museum. Details and colors skittered in my head.

The door of my room opened slowly. A hand held out a china doll with pink lips and bright, azure eyes frozen open. Her blonde ringlets were swept up in a rose -colored ribbon. A high-pitched voice came from behind the door.      "I jumped straight out of the toy-store window, just so I could be yours." The doll head bobbed, and her eyes closed.   My heart leapt for joy!   I knew it was my father, and I was beyond relieved, but I wasn't going to let on.

"Okay, Papa, you can come in," I said.

My father opened the door wide. I threw myself into his arms, the doll crushed between us.

"I couldn't come or write, Maddie. I'm so sorry."

"You are safe!" The doll dropped to the floor.

Now I've never had a doll so fine, and didn't have the heart to tell him that at that moment, I couldn't have cared less.  I picked up the frozen-faced thing.

"I wish you were a little girl still wrapped in your mama's arms by the fire," he said. "I wish this terrible war had never started. I watched men I'd come to love die in front of me."   "Oh, Papa." I held him like he was the child and I was the adult. *In that moment as I watched my father weep, how could I tell him I was waiting for . . . something? And for the first time in my life, wishing him to leave?*

He drew back, wiping his eyes, and looked at me, at the different me.  "My regiment will remain here, Maddie, at one of the forts that guard the city. I don't know how often I can get away, what with rumors of a Rebel invasion, and—"

"The doll is really pretty, Papa." I didn't know what else to say.

"Maddie, you must promise me never, never to run off again. Salome said you gave her such a fright."

"I can't promise that, Papa," I said.

"Maddie! What has happened to you? Where is my good little girl, my darling?"

"She's gone, Papa!"

I went to the window and looked out at the alleyway below. I was trying to think what else to say to my father when I saw two large, white men in overalls hovering at the doorway to the kitchen. One carried a rope, the other a shotgun. They were slave catchers, I was nearly certain.   I had to warn Nellie. And if Isaac was about? My God!

I had to leave right then. "Papa! I forgot! I have to finish helping Aunt Salome. She counts on me, she—" I pushed past him. "Leave me alone!"I raced through the hall, and down to the kitchen. Nellie was kneading dough, punching it hard. "Men! Strangers outside, Nellie!"   Nellie stopped cold. "Mm hm," she said, and calmly walked to a wooden enclosure at the corner of the kitchen where the slops buckets were stored. She hefted a full one and dragged it to the door leading to the alley. She opened it and sure enough, the men still lurked there.   Without a word, Nellie emptied the bucket of waste, and the slime of it flooded the doorway. The men backed away.   "Watch your slops, mammy!" one said.

"I'm dreadful sorry, suh," Nellie answered, head bowed. She backed away muttering her sorrys until she'd closed the door.     Without a word, Nellie returned to her task of kneading, only now her punches grew harder as she slammed both fists into the mass of dough. I watched as Nellie rolled the bread makings into a large ball and dropped it into a pan. She poured water over her hands, wiped them off on a towel, and picked up a quilt from under the wooden counter. It was the same one she'd hung in the window to the alley after she'd caught me alone outside. It was of rough, heavy texture with red zigzag stripes embroidered across it. At the bottom were two half-moon shapes.

Nellie hung the quilt in the window from a large, brass hook.     "Ain't nobody in the cellar," she said to me. "Ain't gonna be for a time." With that, she touched my face gently.   I left her there.

There was no sign of my father. I felt beyond relieved that he was safe, and really, really guilty about the ungrateful way I'd behaved.

I was so caught up in these thoughts I didn't see Mr. Webster pacing in the parlor when I walked in.

He motioned for me to come closer. "Do you know how to use a gun?" he whispered.

"Oh, yes, sir." *Yes I did, and why was I feeling so excited by his question? Did this mean he trusted me?*

Mr. Webster looked around to make sure we were alone. He opened a travel bag and pulled out a long, brown shawl. "It has a pocket, here, where it would drape over your arm," he said.

He pressed a small pistol into my hand.

"I have my own, sir."

"You amaze me, miss," he said. "Keep yours hidden in case of trouble. Use the one I'm giving you now."

I put the weapon in the shawl pocket, my hand just over it.

"It's loaded," he said.

## Thirteen

We had walked a few long blocks into a part of the city I'd never seen before. I smelled wood smoke, horse dung, and heavy, cheap perfume. Some women were draped in doorways wearing nothing more than a chemise and petticoats. Others were beckoning from windows, with curtains half drawn. A few scantily dressed, boldly painted women with bright red lips and rouged cheeks clustered about some soldiers, laughing and pocketing money. Others looked gaunt and hungry, with ragged children at their skirts. Most watched us as we passed.

"Keep your hand on the weapon," Mr. Webster said, walking close beside me. "This place is known as Swampoodle. It is dangerous, always." He guided me through a maze of narrow walkways past Negro shanties, old men puffing corncob pipes and women with brightly colored bandanas wringing out wash. A group of corralled cattle—their calves nearly buried beneath them—were packed tight, mooing and lowing.

"They're on their way to the slaughterhouse," Mr. Webster said, as one of the cows with long-lashes and soft sad eyes stared at me. "It is a hungry army, hungry to kill and hungry for food."

I reached through the slats of wood that held the animals and stroked the soft, black nose of a little calf.

"No time for sentiment, Miss Bradford," Mr. Webster said. "Watch where we are going."

We wound through those foul-smelling streets at least five times, never stopping. Was Mr. Webster trying to confuse me? I was a bit nervous, but mostly I was wrapped up in storing what I was seeing in my head. Perhaps Mr. Webster wanted me to remember every turn, every shabby door front, every face I'd seen. That, as you know, was easy for me.

We walked further, at least another mile. At last, we came to a street. It was clean, almost serene, with a small park and a grove of leafy oak trees.

A few children played, spinning tops, pitching horseshoes. Their mothers or governesses sat knitting or chattering close by.

"I'll leave you now," Mr. Webster said.

*"Why?" Would he leave me alone? Here, in the middle of a strange city that crackled and smelled, and hummed and unnerved me?*

"Stay right here on this bench. Someone will contact you very shortly. You'll be addressed by the name of Fiona. Remember that. Wait for that." He looked at the children, and sighed deeply. "That little tyke with the brown hair and gap-toothed smile," he said softly. "My only son . . . there is, was, a resemblance. I've missed out, you see, He's a man now, and has no idea what I do." I saw a mist of tears forming in his eyes. But not for long. He blinked and drew up straight, alert like a hunting dog waiting for a quail to fly out of a bush. "Remember to stay right here, Miss Bradford."

As Mr. Webster was leaving, he stopped to pick a bunch of buttercups. He held them to his nose, then, disappeared into the grove of trees.

I too watched the children, their faces like flowers as they darted about, singing, tussling in the sunlight. I was never that carefree, I thought. Never.

What would happen next?

An elderly woman carrying a cloth bag lowered herself with some difficulty onto the bench next to me. She had sparse, silver hair that peeked from a wide-brimmed straw hat.

"I've none of my own," she said. "Little ones, that is. I could watch them all day." She rummaged in her bag, her hands stiff and gnarled.

"My knitting needles, might you help me get them out, dear? I'm making a sweater for one of those girl-children, any one of the bunch. I've named them all Amy after my dear sister who left this earth sixty-seven years ago. Or was it last week?"

She looked at me with milky, clouded-over blue eyes.

"Amy, is that you?"

I found her needles and put them in her hands. "No, ma'am. I'm not Amy." Was this the woman who would call me Fiona?

"Yes, you are Amy!" she shouted, holding her hands over her ears.

Just then, a rubber ball hit me square on my arm. I caught it, looking for the child who might have thrown it.

He was next to me in a wink: A tiny boy wearing a black slouch cap pulled down to his nose grabbed the ball from me.

"You'll get a spanking surely for that, Mikey!" a woman called out, coming straight toward us. She was red-haired, slender, and small, not young or old, wearing a blue bonnet and a simple, gray dress. "

You scared me silly. Come along, now, Fiona, Mikey, the both of you!"

*Fiona! The name Webster told me someone would use. Fiona.*

The boy trotted obediently to the woman's side. "Sorry, Mama," he piped in a high squeaky voice.

"You foolish girl." She pointed at me. "You were supposed to be watching over him!" she snapped. "Come with me, Fiona." I hesitated, "Now!" she said. I got up to follow her.

When we were just outside the park, she reached into her pocket and pulled out several coins. She dropped them into the boy's hand. He picked one up, and bit down hard on it. "They're beauties!" he said, smiling broadly, showing a set of uneven, stained teeth. He pulled up his pant leg and shoved the coins into his sock. Only then did I see he was not a true boy at all. He was a young man, no more than

78

three feet tall, with hairy legs, and tiny, and calloused hands. "Thanks, Mike," the woman said. He doffed his hat to her.

"You got distracted, rummaging into that old woman's bag," she said sharply to me. "She was no threat, but you didn't know that. Listen well, girl. You will never, never know if someone is a true danger. You must be alert and on guard at all times. Expect the unexpected. This is a battlefield. Do you understand?" Her tone was harsh.

"Yes, ma'am," I said, berating myself silently. I never thought that anyone, anytime, anywhere might be an enemy. "I'll learn, I swear it." I would.

"I'll report that to my . . . superior," she reached out to shake my hand. I took it. Her grip was so tight my hand was growing numb. "I could have thrown you to the ground," she said. "Don't ever shake the outstretched hand of a stranger."

"I won't."

"Good. At least you stood your ground." She let me go.

"Take us back to Swampoodle, Miss Fiona," Mikey ordered.

*Swampoodle. I retraced our steps back, back into my mind. Try to remember the way.*

I made a sharp turn, my head rattling with the right directions. I wound around the foul streets; tracking backwards just the way Mr. Webster had taken me. Mikey and the woman watched me closely as I moved with growing assurance.

Finally, a Union soldier with flabby cheeks and a dead-set, grim face moved in front of us so we could not take another step. Mikey extended two fingers of his hand, keeping the other close to his side. With a flutter of his eyes, the soldier acknowledged him and led us to a storefront with heavy wooden doors. The sign in the window read

**Dr. Josiah Swain's Oils and Nostrums: Cures for the Feeble and the Loveless. By Appointment Only.**

Inside we passed by three more guards, down a short, empty hallway to a room so thick with cigar smoke that at first, no one was visible inside. A telegraph machine whirred in the corner. Next to it was a man's form shrouded in smoke and darkness. A single oil lamp, lit low, sat on a desk heaped with papers.

The man padded across the room with heavy slippers that flapped and flopped with each step. He was brown-bearded, with a slice of gray at the top and a full bottom lip peeking out from just under his face-hair. A lit cigar sat in a ready cleft in the corner of his mouth where it wagged like a tail. As he neared, I saw his vest was covered with white ash.

"Let us have illumination!" he said in a loud voice.

"Yes, sir," Mikey answered. Lamplight flooded the room. I could see then that the man had the eyes of a hawk; gold and brown with spots of black near the irises.

The woman who'd accompanied me sat down in a chair, next to someone else who remained in shadow, still, like a bird on its perch. "This is the wee bairn you bring me, eh, Mike?" The man spoke with a thick, Scottish burr.

"Yes, sir. This is the kid," Mike replied. I bristled at being called a kid, especially by someone who was at least a foot shorter than I was.

"Mr. Pinkerton, she is indeed remarkable," Mr. Webster said, stepping from the corner of the room, He spoke in the same proper accent he'd used before with me, minus any trace of a Southern drawl. I knew surely then it was his true voice, as he was obviously among his own kind.

Mr. Pinkerton! I was actually standing before the great detective himself! I was thrilled, and nervous. I swallowed, trying to summon words. My hands, wet with perspiration, clutched at my skirts.

"Describe the painting you saw in the Smithsonian, lass," Pinkerton ordered. "Every detail. Now." I breathed in and out. Okay, you can do this, I told myself. And then it came to me. Be someone else. Remember when I told you about how I'd do that kind of pretending after my accident? I did it then. I imagined myself like this: Elegant, graceful, smiling, a perfect Southern lady.

I relaxed my body. My hands that normally hung by my sides with little grace in their movements shaped and arranged to flow and curve, moving lightly as I spoke—in a refined Southern accent, just like Mr. Webster had when we first met.

"Well, sirs and ma'ams," I said, fluttering my eyes, "in the painting, there were three Indian warriors. The one in the lead was called Black Knife. On his head he wore a white feather tipped in black, sticking out from the top of a brown headdress that fell over his ears." I paused, but barely, wiping at my eyes, as the cigar smoke wound over my face. "Black Knife's eyes, as I faced the painting, looked to the right, the same hand rested on his thigh held a thin, wooden spear. His mount looked to the left, a glorious steed with brown coloring from the hoof to the knee, and a black mane, tail, and legs." I paused, lowering my head, arranging my newly graceful hands in my lap, a position I'd never assumed before. Mr. Pinkerton shifted his cigar to the other corner of his mouth; a pile of ashes fell to

t

h

e

f

loor. Without taking his eyes from my face, he rubbed at them with his foot.

"Continue," he said. "The sky in the painting, sir, was cloudy, muddled, fire smoke, perhaps, except for a burst of light in the background, like there was an inferno behind them. There was a jagged tree bottom just to the left of Black Knife. Behind him were two other Indian braves. One had his right hand just above his eyes, peering in that same direction. About one yard or so, just at his rear, came the last man, both hands on his reins. They approached a split in a rocky ridge. There you have it, sirs," I glanced at the women, "and madams." A last flutter of my eyes as the Southern belle I'd become disappeared in the cigar smoke.

Mike whistled and hollered, "Whoeee! That was fine!" I stood tall, speaking in my normal voice. "I am Madeline Eve Bradford from Portsmouth, New Hampshire, the daughter of Private Summoner Bradford of the $2^{nd}$ New Hampshire Infantry, as you know, one of the first regiments to answer the call." "I'm well aware of who you are, lass," Pinkerton said. My words were spilling out now. "And I want to work for you, sir. I think I know how the Rebels got their intelligence before the battle of Bull Run." I was running low on breath.

"Really, and I suppose the sun is green, then?" Mr. Pinkerton said, with no

s
m
i
l
e

at all. I faced him full on. As I mentioned, I'm a bit taller than average.      There was a long pause as he slowly folded a bright plaid hanky over a large stain on the collar of his shirt. "What was the Rebel courier's name?"

"Her name was Betty Duvall. I saw her three times. In the alley she called the man who took the packet Colonel Jordan—"

"You heard the name clearly?" Mr. Pinkerton asked. "Are you certain?" His raptor eyes held mine.

"Oh, yes, sir. I hid behind a woodpile. They were both armed. He removed an object from her loosened hair in an alley behind the house at 1625 K Street."

"Who lives in the house?" Pinkerton demanded.

"Mrs. Rose Greenhow, and she's a Rebel too, but you well know that, sir."

Mr. Pinkerton puffed harder on his cigar. I was a bit nauseated from the fumes, but kept talking.

"Betty went straight to that house and was loudly addressed by Mrs. Greenhow as Amanda," I said. "I believe Betty is her real name."

I paused. Images rushed through my head, and tumbled from my mouth.

"When the door opened, there was a little girl holding a rag doll next to Mrs. Greenhow. The doll's petticoat was red. Moments later someone placed it in the window. The petticoat color had changed to blue. I don't know if that is important, or—"

"Did ye hear all that, Mrs. Warn?" Pinkerton asked.

"How do we know that this, this child didn't just imagine these things?" the silent woman answered. Mrs. Warn, he called her. I remembered how she'd earlier appeared next to me when I was with Mr. Webster. And how she'd berated me for my carelessness.

"I was right there, ma'am. And I'm going on sixteen, hardly a child."

"I believe her, Mrs. Warn," Mr. Webster said.

"As do I. And there's an end on it, madam." Mr. Pinkerton took her by the arm into a corner of the room and whispered something in her ear.

"There's more," I said. "I dressed as a man and made my way to my father's camp just before his regiment moved to Centreville. I, we, followed them."

"We?"

"A boarder at my aunt's house. Actually *he* followed *me*."

"His name?" Mr. Pinkerton asked—demanded, really.

Would this bring Jake trouble? I stopped short of telling them. "When we were heading toward a ridge overlooking Manassas, we saw part of the battle. Betty Duvall rode past us, back toward Washington City. She was galloping hard, sir."

"Who is the *we* you speak of?" Pinkerton's voice boomed.

I hesitated.

"Who?" He shouted louder.

"I believe his name is Jake," I said, hoping that would end it.

"His last name!"

I looked to Webster for help. "Whitestone," he said. "I know the young man, I board in the same house. He is a reporter for the *New York Tribune*."

I caught my breath. They knew about Jake. Did everyone? The next time I saw him, I would tell him off, I would—I . . . I didn't know what I would do . . . If I saw him again.

"Good! That paper is a friend to the Union, as in all probability is the young reporter. Keep me apprised," said Mr. Pinkerton. "And you, Miss Bradford, did you pass easily as a man?"

"Oh, yes, sir," I answered, trying to clear my mind, rid it of Jake White-stone's face, and eyes—

"How well do you shoot?" Pinkerton asked. Without waiting for an answer, I slid the revolver from the shawl pocket. At that moment, Mike threw a tobacco tin up in the air.

"Mind the cat!" Pinkerton snapped. I did not flinch. I fired. The bullet struck the tin. It tumbled through the air, and landed on the floor.        I lowered the weapon.

"I hope the cat is all right, sir," I said. "I like cats."

"Well done, indeed," said Pinkerton, a hint of a smile on his face.

Of course, there never was a cat.

"Spot on!" shouted Mike.

Mr. Pinkerton touched the scar on my forehead. "An unusual mark, rather like a comet, eh? How did that happen?"

"I was six years old, sir," I said quickly. "I fell out of a tree."

*Nancy called to me, so I teased a limb with my weight, and when I fell I felt a rush of wind and a freedom, like I was flying. But when I landed, Nancy wasn't there. Just me, broken; my head smashed on a river rock.*

"Once I made myself a pair of wood and paper wings," Mr. Pinkerton said. "Fell straightway into a neighbor's barn, smack down on a cow. She lived. But oh, how I did soar, briefly."

He smiled at me. "By the by, did you know that the name Fiona means lovely?"

"No, sir, I did not."

"Scottish name, of course. Coined by the poet James McPherson, and chosen by Mr. Webster, even though he is English born." Mr. Pinkerton smiled fondly at Mr. Webster.

"It suits you, Miss Bradford," Webster said, "As will other aliases, should you measure up."

"We'll just see about that," Mrs. Warn snapped.

"You are heard, madam!" Mr. Pinkerton glared at her. He took me by the shoulders. "Miss Bradford, if you pass muster"—he glanced back at Mrs. Warn—"with *all* of us, it will be one assignment at a time, nothing permanent. And you can tell no one, not even your father what you are doing. Do you understand me?

"Yes, sir."

"You are very young, and while you have remarkable abilities, this work of ours is deadly serious. If we're caught, any laws of war do not protect us. The penalty for spying is imprisonment or hanging. Do you hear me?"

Did I? *As much as I could, standing there excited beyond measure in that cigar-choked room with my head buzzing and my heart a-tilt. But did I want to be a part of them? Do something really worthwhile? Yes!*

"Yes, sir. I understand."

"Give her a clerkship," Mrs. Warn said, and strode from the room.

Mr. Pinkerton traced the scar on my forehead with his finger. "We may need to paint that over . . . on occasion," he said.

83

Fourteen

Mr. Webster escorted me back to the boardinghouse. On the way, I asked if we might stop at the paper seller to buy, you guessed it, the *New York Tribune*. As we walked, I read "Pan's" latest dispatch. If I muttered angrily, Mr. Webster seemed not to notice. And surely, even the great spy that he was, he couldn't hear the fluttering of my heart as I thought of Jake: His eyes, his hair, his, well, everything.

**Special Dispatch from the *New York Tribune*     In a few days with any luck, I'll be behind the lines. With some assistance, I've managed to gain access to one of General Beauregard's aides, a man I met at the Willard Hotel, shortly after I arrived in the capital. We talked a bit over brandy and milk punch just before the unholy battle just days ago, before men fought and died for the flags they held dear. This goodly gent greeted me as one of the "Bohemian Brigade," as we newspapermen call ourselves. He assures me that I will be safe. And so I will be. So as part of a "brigade" I march forward at last. After all, both sides need the news of the day, do they not? And aren't we "Bohemians" neutral? No, you say? You would be right.**
     **Onward.     PAN**
Didn't he write beautifully? Did I worry for him? What do you think?

We were alike in a way, Jake and I, recording what we'd seen and done, writing about the dips and dangers of our lives. And maybe, now, I might well have an occupation too. I was ready for whatever happened next. At least I thought I was.

                    *

A day and one night passed. Then, I got an assignment!

"You must listen for the signal—sharp, short whistles, in threes, a ninety-count pause, and then three more whistles," Mr. Webster said as we huddled by the fireside. "Come down the front steps, straight to the southwest corner. I'll be waiting."

I waited, too. And waited. I was cleaning my aunt's cherished old ceramic tureen (we'd mended it after the poor old colonel fell on it) and Nellie was waxing the table when I heard the signal, the sharp piercing whistles over the cries of the rag picker and the oysterman. I began counting the seconds.

"I'm going for a stroll with Mr. Webster, Aunt Salome," I called out as she was in the next room. "He promises to show me the Capitol again today."

I counted twenty-five seconds. "Nellie, is all well?" I whispered to her. "Has Isaac been here?"

"No. Things is steady for now."

"Thank goodness," I said.

"And you, Miss Madeline, don't take no Rebel guff from that cotton man, Webster." She looked into my eyes. "Or is this about something else?"

"No. Yes. I can't say, Nellie."

I counted sixty seconds.

"The Capitol building? What do you want to see that unfinished pile of scaffolding for?" Aunt Salome called out, as I grabbed up my bonnet and cloak. I'd only seen it from a distance. With its missing dome, it looked like an old nobleman who'd got his best top hat squashed under the wheels of a carriage. "Be back by supper, Madeline. Your chores are waiting."

"Yes, ma'am," I answered, hoping she wouldn't come into the room.

I counted ninety seconds. Then there they were, the three whistles!

In my haste, as I swept on my shawl, the fringe caught on the darn old tureen, rolling it on its side like a beached whale until it hit the floor, and smashed to pieces.

"What broke? Nellie? Madeline?" As my aunt was coming through the door, I ran past her. "Oh, not my precious tureen!" she cried.

"It slipped out of my hand what has the stiffness, Missus Salome. I'm frightful sorry," Nellie said.

"No pay for a week, you clumsy thing!" I heard my aunt yell.

"She didn't do it! I did! Stop blaming her!" I shouted. Before my aunt could catch me, I fled the house.

Fifteen

I found Mr. Webster on the street corner. He glared at me. "Three seconds late. Don't let that happen again."

"Yes, sir." I didn't tell him I'd yelled at Aunt Salome when she blamed Nellie for what I broke. I hated my aunt for that.

Mr. Webster was out of his usual planter's whites, back to his clergyman's guise. His eyes were fixed on the Greenhow house.

"Seconds are crucial, timing is crucial," he said. "These Rebels are like scorpions, and this city is their battlefield."

The air was thick and so hot; I had a bit of trouble breathing.

"Can you endure this work?" He studied me.      "Yes," I answered, and in spite of the sweat running down my face, never so sure of anything in my life. I followed him past the Greenhow house. He stopped at a flower stand just beyond it. Webster plucked a pink rose from an assortment tucked like bright jewels in a basket. The flower-seller was an older man with a round, pink, jowly face. He wore a yellow felt slouch hat. He had a large white gardenia flower in his lapel. He took the pink rose from Mr. Webster and handed him a white one.

Mr. Webster nodded to the flower-seller.

"Mrs. Greenhow knows she's being watched," he told me. "Sometimes we speak the language of flowers." He tipped his hat to the flower-seller and handed him two double eagle coins.

"All our scrutiny doesn't seem to matter, that's the devil of it. She's been able to get her dispatches out right under our noses. Back before the secession, Colonel Thomas Jordan ran the Rebel espionage ring here in the city. Now he's passed the responsibility to her. And she thrives. Jordan gets Greenhow's reports to the Confederates."

"Through Betty," I said.

"Yes, and likely others. Greenhow consorts with men of power to the lowliest butcher to achieve her ends. We need to get someone into that house, someone she won't suspect. The right person, of course."

The door of Mrs. Greenhow's house opened. A small woman in a maroon gown and straw sunbonnet walked down the stairs, fanning herself.      "That's not Betty," I said quickly.      "Tell me why it isn't her?" He spoke rapidly, demanding an answer.

"Betty is taller and is graceful, even when she flounces like a peacock. This other woman, well, she is much stouter and waddles, putting weight on both her feet at once, like she has something heavy in her skirts. She is past middle-age, as there is a roundness in her back common to older women."      "Might she not have suffered an accident?" Mr. Webster said. "How are you sure of her age?"

"One side of her bonnet has been torn. There is a patch of gray hair peeking through." "Good," said Webster. Before I could soak up Mr. Webster's praise, someone was right next to me, seeming to materialize out of the air.

"She's hardly fit, this girl. I could have harmed her and been gone in an instant," the woman said, her face not visible under a large, feathered hat. I stiffened at her rudeness. Something about her was familiar . . . "We don't need her. He doesn't need the likes of her," she said.

Yes, I knew the voice. It was the woman Mr. Pinkerton called Mrs. Warn.

"I'm to tell you we make the Greenhow arrest the morning after next," she told Webster, pushing in front of me. "Whether we have her courier or not." With that, she was gone. "Never let anyone get that close to you again," Webster said. "Even in a crowd, keep one hand at your side, your revolver close, and learn to spot even a hazy shadow out of the corner of your eye." "Yes, sir." I was flushed from the heat and humiliation. Had I failed already? Mr. Webster offered no comfort. He never did. That was part of his method. He was an amazing teacher without making the lessons obvious. Hard as it was, I learned to mask my feelings. I could not show fear or distress. That would make me vulnerable, and put me, put them all, at risk.

"Do you know who that was, Miss Bradford?" I knew he expected an immediate answer. "That lady was Mrs. Warn. I recognized her from my meeting with Mr. Pinkerton."

"Yes!" Mr. Webster said. "Good." Oh, how I basked in that small praise from him. For just an instant, of course. "Mrs. Warn was the first woman Mr. Pinkerton ever hired on, a remarkable accomplishment in itself. Mr. Pinkerton tasked her over and over until he knew she was ready. It was she who accompanied Mr. Lincoln on the train from Baltimore. Mr. Pinkerton believed she helped to save the President's life. She has prized that, and him," Mr. Webster said. "Mrs. Warn is not easy with other women." As he spoke, he never looked straight at me. He was always watching the street and passersby without seeming obvious.

I watched all about me, too, but I could not help thinking about Mrs. Warn. Was she married, or a widow? Or was she a single woman making her way in a difficult trade? I knew that women had no true rights and were considered their husband's property. Mostly they roll bandages and pie dough, and bear children. I decided I'd rather be someone independent and forceful like Mrs. Warn, no matter how tough I had to learn to be.

"Are you managing to evade your aunt, Miss Bradford?" Mr. Webster asked.

"Do you suspect my Aunt Salome, Mr. Webster? Is that why you board with her?" He chuckled. "Would that it could be that easy. Your aunt is a Rebel sympathizer, like over half the people in this city. That is distasteful but hardly dangerous. Her boarding house was convenient, as she is so close to the Greenhow place."

I wondered if he knew what else went on in Aunt Salome's house as I thought about brave, furious Isaac, the escaped slaves, and Isaac's mother's complicity. My dear Nellie. I'd grown to care for her so.

"You'll not see me in the morning," he said. "I cross the lines to Richmond tonight." "How will you do that, cross the lines? What route do you take?"

He didn't answer that. It was impudent of me to ask. It was likely a secret route. Was I growing too brash? Should I tell Mr. Webster that he was important to me, and that I was blooming in his keep? I didn't say anything. I must have been really red as a tomato, though. He offered me his arm. "Drink cold tea, often. The air in the swamp that is this city sickens even the strong. And continue to justify your absences," he said. He was in silent rumination as we walked. As was I, remembering a song I'd heard once from my mother, and once only: *Silent as daybreak Just as bright She will not perish this dark night. Light and ready, this bold maid, is dueling danger in the glade —* I stopped short. Betty, the rebel courier, was stopped near an omnibus. She was smiling broadly, her gloved hands resting on the reins of a man on a huge, dappled stallion.

I decided to call her by name, and if she responded, Mr. Webster could make a positive identification. But I didn't want her to see my face. I pulled my shawl nearly over my head. "Betty!" I cried, in a high-pitched child's voice, rushing toward her. She stiffened, and then quickly turned away, the smile leaving her face in a flash. The man on the horse was Colonel Jordan. He spurred the animal hard, gripping a sword at his side that was sheathed in an ornate leather covering.

"Best pray they did not see your face. They'll be followed," Webster said. "Now you have identified them. Good, very good."

"What now, sir?" I asked, proud and worried all at once.

"Go back home right now. I don't want you to be a familiar figure at this location." In a rare gesture of affection, he patted my hand. "You're a very special girl indeed." Before I could answer or thank him, or turn absolutely scarlet, he was off.

Sixteen

That night things got really scary. It was no kid's dream about monsters like the kind I used to have back in Portsmouth, when I thought witches with puckered faces and arms like tentacles were reaching for me. This one was real.

I stepped out to use the privy. Before I reached it, someone grabbed me from behind, ripped away my shawl and the gun with it. Before I could make a sound, a gag was in my mouth. I kicked and struggled against my captor, but was no match. Strong arms, like bands of metal, held me fast. I was dragged me away, my feet flopping like a cloth doll. Sickly sweet scents of gardenias, violets and musky tuberose flooded my nostrils. My stomach heaved.

I was forced into the back of a carriage, blindfolded, and thrown face down on the seat. A gun barrel was pressed to my temple. I could hear the snorting of a horse, and smelled the sharp tang of linseed-oiled leather.

"Stay still, Yankee brat!" A rough, guttural voice was close to my ear. My hands were tied with a rope so they were nearly straight out in front of me. The carriage was moving. I could sense that there were two people in the cab of the conveyance, one on either side of me. There must have been a driver, too, because I heard the snap of reins as the horse went faster.

I forced my breathing to slow as the gag made me gasp for air. It was fear I felt, sure, but more than that. I felt anger, a hot steady anger at the Rebels who'd captured me. I would not die like this!

I counted seconds, then minutes. Finally the carriage stopped. I was lifted into the strong captor's arms and carried up some stairs. I kicked hard again. My boot slammed into someone's leg.

"Damn you!" It was another voice, a female one. I heard a bell sound three times. There was a rush of air as a door opened.

I could hear low murmurings in a hallway that stopped as soon as I was carried past.

Another door opened. I was pushed into a room down onto a carpeted floor that smelled of pomade, rust, and musk oil perfume. No light from the room was visible though my blindfold. The door closed with a thud, followed by the sound of a lock clicking shut.

I struggled to my feet, my bound hands in front of me. I groped around the room, feeling for any furnishings, any other doors. Nothing.

I heard a knocking. What in heaven's name was happening?

"Yes?" I answered. There was silence. "Who's there?" I tried to keep my voice low and calm. Another knock. I fumbled my way to the door. I groped around it, feeling for a knob. The door was flat. No knob. There was no way to open it. Now what?

Suddenly the door swung open, nearly smacking me in the face. Before it closed there was enough light through my blindfold to see that a female form had come into the room carrying a lamp and a stool. Her head was down so I couldn't see her face.

"Sit," she ordered. I stayed right where I was. She put the lamp on the floor. She grabbed my shoulders and forced me to the stool.

"What is your name?" I raised my head. "Don't look up." She spat the words. "Answer!" She grasped my chin, pulling off the gag.

My hands were sweating and my wrists were getting numb from the tight, tight binding. Someone else was in the room. I smelled gardenias, and strong tobacco.

"We've captured your father," a man said.

My hands shook. I willed them to stop. Dear God, my father . . .

"Sergeant Summoner Bradford. Of the 2$^{nd}$ New Hampshire. Those cowards ran like rats in fire smoke at Bull Run." His voice was slow, deliberate, and now, in my ear.

"He did not run!" I was shouting. "Don't you dare hurt him. Keep me, and let him go. He knows nothing about —"

The woman chuckled. "Do you know a Yankee spy called Timothy Webster?" she demanded.

"No!" I shouted. Mr. Webster was known to them. My God.

"Liar!" she hissed.

"What do we do with her?" the man asked.

"She'll talk after I'm done," the woman said. "If not, shoot her."

I heard them leave the room. Again, the door closed and locked. If they were going to kill me, I'd give them a fight! I waited, hearing my heart beating in my ears. I twisted my hands against the rope, but they wouldn't come free.

At least twenty minutes passed by my count. The air grew more stifling. What was happening? Would I be here forever?

I lowered myself to the floor. I pitched and rolled and bucked my body up and down along the floor.

When I reached the door, I kicked it with both of my legs. It didn't move. What next? My hair was tied back with a velvet ribbon and a wide-toothed comb fastened the rest. I shook my head furiously until the comb fell out. I grabbed it in my mouth and continued my thrashing. Finally, my wrists burning and raw, I freed one of my hands from the rope by twisting them. I tore off the blindfold and slid my other hand free. The room was so dark. I held the comb to my eyes, and broke it, leaving a long, sharp piece.

I heard footsteps. Someone was approaching. The door opened. I raised the jagged comb. As a man came in, I stepped in front of him. He grabbed my hand, twisting it, but not before I stabbed the comb into his wrist. He cried out in pain.

"Enough!" a woman shouted. I heard the door swing open.

Suddenly the room was flooded with lights.

I blinked hard, dizzy and nauseated. I tried to run but smacked right into a large cart, piled with food. Cakes, sandwiches and a teapot crashed to the floor.

I saw that the woman binding the man's bleeding hand with my blindfold was Mrs. Warn! Two other women stood there, smiling. One was older, fair-haired and wore silver-rimmed spectacles. The other was small with red hair. I recognized her. She was the woman from the park, the one who called me Fiona. What was happening?

I may sound calm now in the telling, but I swear I was so stunned by what I was seeing that my head whirled, and my knees were so wobbly that I could hardly remain standing. *Don't take it all in at once*, I told myself. *Focus on one person at a time. Try to calm down.*

I looked at Mrs. Warn. *Focus hard,* I said to myself. Remember I'd never really seen her face until then. It was narrow, her chin and cheekbones prominent, her lips full but at that moment, set in a hard line. She had wide set blackish-brown eyes that looked like they were shooting sparks straight at me. She was wearing a plain black frock with an embroidered lace collar. Mrs. Warn didn't look like a powerful woman at all. She looked like a little brown wren. Her hair was up and fastened in a wilted chignon. She was shorter than I remembered.

"Tea is waiting, dears," the older lady said, salvaging what she could from the mess on the floor. "I'm Agnes Crawford," she said to me, "and of course you know Jane Smith from the park." Jane Smith? A name as common as a dust speck, I thought. An alias, likely. "And perhaps you've seen Mr. Riley, or bought some of his lovely blossoms?" In spite of the fact that I'd just stabbed him, the man she called Mr. Riley smiled at me. The scent of blossoms that emanated from him was overpowering and I knew then that he was the flower-seller just near the Greenhow house.

"Good work, miss," Mr. Riley said, the cloth on his hand now stained with blood.

Mrs. Crawford went breezily on. "And Mrs. Warn you've met, of course."

"I'm sorry I hurt you," I said to Mr. Riley, ignoring Mrs. Warn.

"Don't be," Mrs. Warn said. "Don't ever be sorry."

"Just a scratch," Mr. Riley added.

Jane Smith handed me a wet cloth. "Wash up, now, Madeline Bradford, and oh, my, your little wrists are a bit red, aren't they?" She reached into her apron pocket and produced a tiny pot of something creamy. "Put this on the scratches, and they'll be gone by morning." She watched as I rubbed in the ointment. "Better?"

"Yes," I mumbled. They weren't.

"Mrs. Crawford has made some lovely raisin scones," Jane Smith said cheerfully. "Are you hungry?"

"I'm starved, thanks," I said loudly, though my body was cold and I was shaking all over. I hid my trembling hands at my side.

"Good girl," Jane Smith said, clapping me on the back. "Good!"

Mrs. Crawford bustled off, humming. Soon she was back with a new tray of pastries, sandwiches, and a steaming pot of tea. Mr. Riley pulled side chairs and a table from a closet.

Mrs. Warn did not look at me or speak all through the meal. Though the first bite of the scone stuck in my throat, I forced a swallow. Mrs. Warn handed me a sandwich.

"Thank you," I said, meeting her steady, piercing gaze. The salty ham and brown bread looked wonderful. I took a few bites, never taking my eyes off her. Was that a look of approval, admiration, even, on her face?

A bell clanged three times in the hallway. They all looked up, waiting. It clanged twice more. Mrs. Crawford hurried to answer it. I heard laughter, and a loud, "Oh, you rascal!" from Mrs. Crawford, and a high guffaw. She came in, followed by the little man called Mikey. They were laughing like crazy at some silliness they shared.

"Time to go home, Fiona," Mikey said, pulling back my chair. He blew a kiss to Mrs. Crawford, and then danced a little Irish jig, leaping in the air and landing at her feet.

"Oh, the scamp," she said, blushing.

Before we left, Mrs. Warn handed me my shawl and my gun.

"I'll inform Mr. Pinkerton that you . . . tolerated . . . the exercise," she said.

"Do you live here, Mrs. Warn?" I asked. The bit of food I'd eaten, and the realization that they were not really my enemies, made me feel stronger.

"This is Mrs. Warn's school. I'm one of her . . . graduates," Jane Smith said proudly. She indicated the two men sitting in the corner, stuffing more food in their mouths. "And Mike there, well, he's one of our best, as is Mr. Riley."

Mike led me down the stairs of the house I'd been brought to as a captive. I kept blinking in the faint light of dawn. I'd been there all night! If I didn't know better, I would have supposed that a fine, well-bred family lived here. Well, in a way, they were a family, just not like any I could have imagined.

"Well, Fiona, you held your own, and didn't buckle under, that's what I heard," Mike said, skipping along beside me.

"Thanks." I remembered the bile in my throat and the burning in my wrists. My legs were still weak. "I thought I'd been captured by Rebels. I figured they'd kill me."

"And you didn't break," Mike said. "I'm proud of you."

I was proud of myself. "Is Mrs. Warn always so hard on her . . . students?" I leaned down to catch his answer.

"She has to be," he said. "Especially since you're so young, and all. She has to know if you can measure up."

"What about you, Mike?"

"I bless the day Mrs. Warn laid eyes on me," he said, with a tone of reverence in his voice. "She found me working with an organ grinder. I was the monkey. He made me wear an old fur suit and monkey head that stank worse than a rotting horse. When the war started, we'd be just across from the President's House. Those congressmen gave a mighty lot of pennies, and talked real free, talked rebel stuff. They spouted off about who was resigning and who wanted to put a hole in Mr. Lincoln's head. They talked plenty around an animal and his keeper. Mrs. Warn happened by and put an extra penny in my hand. She treated me good, and figured right away I wasn't a real monkey. One day I told her what I was hearing." Mike's face was full of adoration. "A few days later, Mrs. Warn bought me from the organ grinder. He gave me up easy. Money does that. After that, Mr. Pinkerton schooled me in their ways, and took me on. I'd die for them," he said.

As we neared the boardinghouse, a familiar black-haired young man with a bouquet of carnations in his hands limped into the street calling my name.

I gasped.

"Know him, or what?" Mike said, pulling a small knife from under his hat, and concealing it in his hand.

Joy and anger made a broth that bubbled on an invisible stove inside me, just at the sight of Jake Whitestone. "Yes. I do. He boards with my aunt as well."

"Keep walking," Mike said. "I'll be nearby if you need me. Over by Mr. Riley's stand, okay? Go inside."

Hard as it was, I turned my back on Jake and hurried into the house. He followed me.

## Seventeen

"Both of you come and go like stray cats!" Aunt Salome berated me and Jake as Nellie passed us mountains of food. We didn't eat a bite. Jake kept trying to catch my eye. I kept looking away. "Where have you gotten to, Mr. Whitestone? The board is overdue," my aunt said through a mouthful of food.

"Madeline, you've still got the fever. Look at you."

Was my face that flushed?

"Sorry, Mrs. Hutton," Jake said, producing several gold pieces. "I've been rather busy."

She grabbed them up, and bit down on them to see if they were real.

"Excuse me, Aunt," I said, fleeing the table, my heart and head in a tumble. I was so happy to see Jake, and yet, now that I was a spy, I sure didn't want him writing about me in any way, or following me!

I ran into the parlor. He was right behind me. Every time he neared me, I moved away. "Don't use me anymore in your writing! Think for yourself," I whispered.

He winced. I was sorry to hurt him.

"It wasn't just you I wrote about, Miss Madeline. You are a representation of all poor kids caught up in this mess!" he said.

"Kids? Kids? I'm no kid! Go away!"

"All right, maybe I did use you, but it was for my paper! My Yankee paper! Why did you pretend to not know me in the street, Miss Madeline? And who was that funny looking boy you were with?"

"Nobody! He . . . he is the son of my aunt's friend." Okay, that sounded stupid. "He's someone I know. I was minding him while . . . It's none of your business anyway!" I was trying to think fast and it wasn't working. Jake was too close to me. I moved away.

He grabbed my hand. "Madeline." He said my name softly. So familiar, so—

"Just leave me alone," I said weakly, meaning it and not meaning it. Oh boy, was I in a muddle.

I let go of his hand. There was an empty space where his fingers had clasped mine. I could feel myself going all soft and weak. I had to push him away. So I shouted at him.

"I can't forget that you were smiling at Confederate officers after the battle. I saw you!"

"You mean at the reporters' tent?"

"How should I know what it was?"

"For heaven's sake, I told you before, all of us reporters were interviewing them, trying to get the real news out! Next time it won't be so easy. They were flushed with victory and cheering at news of the Union dead. They were crowing! I hate their kind, you should know that."

All the excitement and jangle of the past weeks flooded over me. There was so much I wanted to tell him, so much. I sighed. My shoulders slumped.

"You look older, Madeline."

"I am."

He touched my face. "What has happened?"

*Nothing much, just my whole life has changed*, I thought.

"Oh, the war and the strange new things about this city, worry for my father, for all the soldiers, the wounded. . ." My voice trailed off. "A lot different from New Hampshire, the heat, the . . ." I was rambling.

"My paper is sending me to Richmond, Madeline."

I felt relief and sadness all at once. I knew I couldn't keep doing well at my new trade easily with Jake in the city. And the spies I'd come to know wouldn't let him be in the way. I wanted to say so much more.

"Godspeed, Pan," I said. "Watch out for alligators."

"They don't have those reptiles in Richmond, at least not the kind with scaly skin and killing jaws. You'll read about my time there."

We stood very close together, not moving or speaking.

I closed my eyes, and for a moment imagined us safe and peaceful on the banks of the Pisqataqua River, an autumn wind whistling through the reeds.

But then I heard the city: The distant rumbling of artillery practice, the screech of a night owl, and the cries of the rag and bone seller as he dragged his cart past the parlor window. Washington City, the ruckus and hum of the place was calling to me. I belonged here.

When I opened my eyes, Jake was gone.

Eighteen

Very late that night, a devilishly dark night it was, I was jarred awake when I sensed a man's form standing over me. I didn't cry out, but turned slowly over on my side, reaching under my pillow where I kept my revolver. He grasped my arm. I drew my legs up under me, preparing to kick. Before I could, or struggle even, he reached under my pillow and drew out my weapon.

"You didn't make a sound, Good." He whispered, handing me the gun, his other hand close to my face.

Unless there were two men in this city with a most peculiar deformity, a crooked pinky finger, well -

"Good evening Mr. Webster," I said softly, trying to breathe evenly to quiet my racing heart.

"Come with me, Miss Bradford. Now."

I was wearing a heavy, cotton, sleeping gown, so I slipped out of bed, and grabbed the first piece of clothing hanging in the wardrobe— my old black dress. Since it was so dark in the room, I abandoned modesty, dropped my gown to the floor and pulled on a pair of under drawers, and slipped the dress over my head. I stepped into my boots, lacing them quickly. Was I in for another test even harder than the one I'd endured?

"I'll have you back by morning," was all he would say.

We tiptoed down the hall, past bedrooms, down the stairs, through the parlor and out the front door. Mr. Webster led me around the side of the house into the alley where a horse and rig waited. The driver, yes, he was really small, perched in his seat like a tiny bird. He tipped his hat to me.

"Hi kid," he said. I glared up at him as Mr. Webster helped me into the rig. So Mike was in on this too.

I knew better than to ask where we were going. At least I was with people I knew and not being dragged off, blindfolded. I leaned back against the cushiony leather back of the carriage to catch my breath.

The city smells and sounds, the babble of drunkards, the clatter of wheels on cobblestones, and the stink of the canals, faded to the scent of dung, grass and fire smoke. We stopped. Mr. Webster got out and walked quickly away. Mike jumped down and held out his hand to help me down.

"You look like something a cat wouldn't drag around." He said, appraising my black garb, and my matted, uncombed hair.

"You don't look so great yourself," I snapped, pointing to his battered bowler hat and pants that barely reached the tops of his little boots. "You sounded just like my Aunt," I muttered. "I never look right to her."

"Sorry. Truce?" He said sheepishly.

We both smiled. I really liked Mike.

I squinted to try to see where we were. Just then, I stumbled over a large, inert mound. It moved, and mooed. I reached down to touch a warm, wet nose of a cow. Nearby I heard the snuffling and grunting of pigs.

A layer of fog hung low over moist, loamy grass. I could barely make out the outline of a large building up ahead.

As we came closer, I realized then we were in front of a barn.

Before I could ask what in heck was going on, a wooden door slid open. A tall Negro man I'd never seen before stood in front of us. He nodded to us.

Mike offered me his arm like he was a fine dandy escorting a lady to a fancy ball. I reached down, I mean I had to really reach down, and took his arm. I entered the building at a crouch, my arm in Mike's.

Through flickering oil lamps positioned all around a cavernous space, men, and yes, women were lifting iron weights, jumping from wooden horses to piles of hay bales on the floor. An arrow sailed over my head and thudded into a target marked with a bulls-eye. In another area of the barn I saw Mr. Riley, the flower seller, hitting a hanging leather bag over and over with his bare hands. He was moving with great agility, like he was dancing, in spite of his bulk. No one greeted me, or looked in the least surprised that I was there.

A small padded form, the face covered by some kind of leather mask waddled over to me.

"Follow me, Miss Bradford," a female voice said from beneath the head covering. She led me to a wooden rack hung with padded jackets, long skirts with no hoops or petticoats and trousers with leather caps over the knees.

"Put these on." While I donned the strange, bulky garments, pulling the skirt over my dress, and sliding my arms into the jacket, the tall Negro man shouted,

"Behind you!" He picked up the smaller female figure and threw her to the floor. She landed hard but slid away with ease.

Before I could move, she leapt up and came toward me, raising her arm as if to strike me. Instinctively, I jumped to the side and grabbed her hand.

She twisted my arm so hard I nearly fainted. I fell flat on my back, gasping.

"Get up!" she said. She repeated the move. This time I grabbed her arm with both hands. "Now, force my arm down, right above my elbow. Keep the pressure on, and push me to the ground. Put your foot on my neck." I hesitated.

"Don't worry about hurting me."

I did as she ordered. And she lay still.

"Release me," she said. When I did, she got up, and removed her head covering. A tumble of reddish hair, and an even redder, sweaty face looked hard at me. It was Mrs. Smith.

103

"Not a bad opponent," she said.

Before I could take in this praise, I saw Mr. Webster put on an overstuffed vest and attach more padding to his legs and a leather cover to his lower area.

As if on cue, Mrs. Smith wheeled around and walked quickly away. As I watched her, someone grabbed me from behind, his hand around my neck. I froze for an instant.

"Kick back hard at his leg!" Mrs. Smith called out. "Don't try to disengage his hand from your neck. He is stronger than you are. Use your elbow in his stomach, then strike between his legs. "

I did, and Mr. Webster crumpled to the ground, groaning loudly.

"Are you all right, sir?"

He stood up, smiling, and brushed himself off. "Quite so. That's why I wore protection. Or else you would have truly hurt me." His smile faded.

"Defending your person is critical. You are well along. Mrs. Smith reported that when they tested you with the fake capture, you defended yourself."

He waved his hand. In an instant the Negro man was at his side. "This is Mr. Oliver Washington, Miss Bradford, one of Mr. Pinkerton's best. Likely you will work together at some point."

"Pleased to meet you, Miss," Mr. Washington said, bowing slightly. He had a deep, melodious voice, brown coffee-colored skin and strong, well muscled arms. One of them was badly scarred.

"Come this way, please." He motioned to a far corner of the barn where a man and a woman were firing guns at a paper cut out of a man.

He handed me a pistol, and bullets.

"Load it. Fire at the head of the target."

I aimed and fired. The bullet landed low and tore into the figure's chest, leaving a black, circle where the heart would have been.

"Just as good, yes." Mr. Washington said.

"Give me the gun." I started to hand it over,

"No. Never give up your weapon."

"Sorry."

"No apologies allowed here, kid." Mike scuttled between Mr. Washington's legs, and grabbed away my gun.

"Again!" Mr. Washington ordered. "If he tries to take the weapon, kick him hard.

"Sure, I can take it." Mike said. I kicked at Mike. He rolled himself up like a dung beetle, righted himself, pulled a knife from his pant leg and came at me.

"Gotcha," he said, jumping in the air, thrusting it at my chest.

By now, the other agents had formed a silent circle around us.

"That's enough for tonight," Mr. Webster said. "You are agile and learn fast, Miss Bradford.

I didn't feel so agile with all those eyes on me. Finally Mrs. Warn approached, her face drenched in perspiration. She reached for my hand, as if to shake it in congratulations. I didn't take it, rather I stepped back until she could no longer reach me.

The group applauded.

"Take her back, now," Mrs. Warn said, a flicker of an expression that was something like approval crossed her face.

"You are not among enemies here," she said. "But you behaved as if you were. Imagine yourself as a panther or a tiger, with knives for claws. Fix images like that in your mind. That is where a lot of power comes from. The mind."

She nodded curtly and walked away.

I think I was proud. Okay, I know I was. And what's more, I didn't want to go back to my aunt's boardinghouse. I wanted a mission!

Nineteen
"

Except for two more training sessions that left me exhausted but knowing I did really well, the next days came and went. Long, chore-filled afternoons blended one into the other. Sometimes it felt like all I'd seen and heard in the past months were but another dream. In the privacy of my room, every morning and evening, I lifted my heavy washbasin over my head fifty times and pushed my self up and down over and over, leaning my weight on my arms. I was determined to make myself even stronger. When I finished, I sat very still and imagined myself a wild, strong animal. If I growled, it was into my pillow, so no one heard me.

Then, one night, when Nellie and I were serving dinner, a tasteless one of boiled turnips and mutton, Aunt Salome was nattering on about how both sides in the war were doing no fighting.

"The Yankees are stuck like hogs in the muck all around the city. Mr. Lincoln sure doesn't know how to run a war." Aunt Salome bustled off, muttering about quicksand.

"Yes, ma'am," I said automatically, not realizing she had gone. I was distracted and anxious. Was there a mission for me, and why did it seem to be taking so long?

Now I've learned to understand that spy missions do not materialize just because you want them to. The waiting can be endless and boring and—

Finally, as I was emptying the dirty washbasin water into the alley, I heard the tread of boots on the cobblestones. I grasped my gun. I'd been in the habit of taking it along whenever I ventured out.

Mr. Webster jumped off a horse and headed straight for me. He looked weary. His boots were mud-stained. "A hard night's ride lashed to the devil's tail, I've had," he said. "But it's not time to rest. Not time." He was speaking quickly and rubbing his eyes.

"Have you any news of Jake Whitestone?" I asked. "I think he's gone to Richmond."

"He arrived safely, that's all I know," Webster said, studying my worried, flushed face. "Don't fix your heart to anyone, Madeline. It's not the time or the place. We've a task for you. But first I must speak with your aunt."

Is that what I had done? Fixed my heart to Jake Whitestone? And had Mr. Webster sensed it? Would that weaken me in his eyes? Or in my own? I'd never had any of these feelings before. No time then. I'd ponder them later, or never.

We found Aunt Salome just as she was retiring to her room.

"Mutton doesn't sit well with me," she said. "What I'd give for a lovely beef roast. Mr. Webster, take your rest. You look like a ghost."

"We'll all feast in style when the Yankee lays down his sword," he drawled.

"Oh, my, with you at my table, Mr. Webster, it will be a fine feast indeed," she said, smiling like a dazzled schoolgirl.

"My dear Mrs. Hutton," he said, "I'd truly like to take Miss Madeline here to stay a day or two with my dear cousin Juliet in Georgetown Heights. She is a fine lady and a friend to our great cause. The air is so much cooler there, and poor little Miss Madeline is looking so pale and thin."

I didn't think I was the least bit pale or thin, but I sighed loudly just the same.

"What with typhoid fever in some parts of the city, I'm sure her father would be so grateful," Webster said.

Grateful? If my father knew that I was probably headed for a spy mission instead of Mr. Webster's "cousin" Juliet's house, he'd be anything but grateful.

Aunt Salome looked relieved. Perhaps the poor lady would be glad to have me out of her keep for a bit.

"That is so kind of you, Mr. Webster," Aunt Salome said, sighing. "I suppose we'll manage somehow. Isn't that kind, Madeline? Of course it is."

106

"Come walk with me, young miss," Mr. Webster said. "Just a brief stroll. The air will do us both good." That was for Aunt Salome's benefit. The days were muggy, and the air was still and hot.

I was dying to ask him what was happening, but I dared not. It was a lesson in itself to walk with him. Knowing how rapidly I took in what was around me, he'd task me over and over. That day his stride was brisk, his eyes straight ahead.

A group of black-faced men in top hats and coat tails ambled by. One blew a trumpet loudly and another crashed a pair of symbols. A third leapt off his feet, and somersaulted to the ground.

"Who are they?" he asked, not breaking his rapid stride,

"I'm not sure, sir, but I do know this: true Negroes they are not. Their faces are painted over with some kind of makeup. But I saw glimpses of white skin around their necks.

"Excellent! They are a band of Mr. Callie's Minstrels, a popular form of entertainment here. Crowds come to see them dancing and singing Negro songs, making a mockery of those good folk for spectator's coins and all the beer they can drink." And as if he'd read my mind, he said, "Did you notice the third man on the left, the tallest of them? He works with us on occasion. That's how our fine agent Mike started. When he was with the organ grinder, sometimes his owner would lend him to a minstrel show. Don't ask Mike how many times he was pelted with beer bottles and oyster shells. Do ask him how much information he gathered about certain Rebels from a few choice moments in the minstrel's dressing rooms."

The image of Mike being hit with bottles made me cringe.

"He'll have much harder times than that. Don't worry for him. He's braver than brave." He did stop then. "You will learn from his example."

"Yes, sir."

"You have been spying. Each time we've walked about, you've been spying. Do you realize that, Miss Bradford? That is what we do, and how we do it. Sometimes it is simple observation. Very good."

I think my grin nearly split my face.

When we'd passed a good few blocks from the boardinghouse, Mr. Webster stopped in front of a storefront, a photograph studio with a hand-lettered freshly painted sign.

**Wishing Well Portrait Makers. Soldiers welcome!**

The store was shuttered then, but by day, I'd seen soldiers crowded into the place to sit like statues in front of the draped camera, while the photographer poured black powder into a pouch, gripped a rubber pump, and froze their faces into a victory smile with a flash and a pop.

Mr. Webster rapped twice on the door, then twice again. The door opened. I followed. Strong odors pervaded the room: Burnt powder, harsh chemical acid, and cigar smoke.

Mr. Pinkerton appeared from behind a curtained doorway and shuffled over to a counter that was piled with glass plates and rolls of paper. He seemed extra preoccupied, extra serious.

"We are placing you inside the Greenhow house, Miss Bradford. We've got word that she has asked for help with her child. You are to be a temporary governess for her daughter, an eight-year-old terror called Little Rose."

Me, take care of a little kid? I had no experience with tending children. And the daughter of a dangerous spy at that!

"Here is how it will work," Mr. Pinkerton said. "Mr. Webster, Mrs. Warn, and Mrs. Smith have cultivated Rebel contacts across the river in Maryland and Virginia, even in Kentucky. Most productive, it has proved to be. They've joined their treasonous organizations, dined at their tables, and passed for one of them."

The pride in Mr. Pinkerton's voice and face when he spoke of Mr. Webster and Mrs. Smith was obvious. Would I ever be thought of in such a way?

Mr. Webster and Mrs. Smith clasped hands. She leaned close to Mr. Webster. I'd never seen men and women display affection like that in public unless they were married or courting. They must have known each other very well indeed. Before I could think too much about such delicate matters, Mr. Pinkerton motioned for me to sit down.

He perched on the arm of my chair. Thankfully his cigar was at that moment unlit so I didn't start choking.

"Some Rebels are known as double agents, helping either side when it suits them. For the right price or some measure of conscience, they sometimes work with us. One of them has done just that in the case of Mrs. Greenhow."

His eyes fixed mine in a gaze so intense; it sent a shiver through me.

"Even though Mrs. Greenhow can't leave her home, knowing she is under constant surveillance, her couriers are passing Union troop intelligence to Confederate officers, as you well know. Mrs. Greenhow will never disclose her methods. She is like a pie safe locked tight. But the daughter, well, we suspect that she has passed on certain codes her mother gives her. You may be able to get information from her."

His expression was one of such loathing that when he lit his cigar with a phosphorous stick, it seemed the very air around him might catch fire too.

"Listen well, lass," Mr. Pinkerton said. "File away all we tell you in that powerful organ of memory you possess, understand?"

"Yes, Mr. Pinkerton." *My brain, my 'powerful organ of memory,' was making a difference!*

"Your name is Lucy Swinton, daughter of Travis Swinton of the 5$^{th}$ Virginia Cavalry. He was gravely wounded at Manassas, and you came to Washington City when you heard he died of his injuries. You were raised in Falls Church, Virginia, right across the Potomac. You have boarded for the past year at Mrs. Elsa Stewarts's Ladies Academy in Richmond, where your late mother, Eliza Swinton, was a distant cousin to Betty Duvall's family. And while you will claim you don't know the courier Betty Duvall, you'll show Mrs. Greenhow this letter from Betty's father, Willard Duvall."

"Mr. Duvall is working with you?" I was beginning to understand how complicated loyalties were, and how Mr. Pinkerton's spies worked to infiltrate the enemy.

"In a manner of speaking. After you identified his daughter Betty to us—and never underestimate how important that was—we were able to find out about her family and use that against her father. We told him we would do our best to see she does not come to great harm."

"He agreed?"

"Oh, yes. He loves his only daughter, yet fears her as well. She shot him in the arm when he prohibited her from joining the Rebel underground. She called him a Negro-loving Lincoln man and left the house."

A girl shooting her own father? I must have looked as shocked as I felt.

"Betty Duvall is a dangerous woman, Miss Bradford."

"How will her father help you?"

"He has agreed to write a letter of introduction to Mrs. Greenhow on your behalf. His late wife was a cousin to Mrs. Greenhow, a woman she's not seen in years."

Mr. Pinkerton handed me the letter.

*My dear Madam Greenhow,*

*Permit this familiarity. While you do not know me, a cousin, my dear late wife, Eliza O'Oneal Swinton by name, was related to you by marriage.*

*I have been an ardent admirer of your patriotism, so to speak, and your bravery.*

*Let this note introduce a fine young woman, Miss Lucy Swinton, a young orphan who has suffered the loss of her father, my old friend Mr. Travis Swinton, at Bull Run.*

*Miss Swinton is well mannered and well educated, and while she is on this solemn and sad visit to Washington City, she would benefit from your support and, perhaps, your guidance. We heard of your desire to have someone as a companion to your precious little Rose while you are enduring such hardships at the hand of the Yankees.*

*Please know that the gentle folk of Falls Church pray for you daily.*
*Time compels me to write in haste.*
*With my own fervent prayer for your continued well being.*
*I am most sincerely,*
*Willard Duvall*

"There is something else you must know, Miss Bradford," Mr. Pinkerton said, looking even grimmer, if that was possible. Mr. Webster put his hand on my shoulder as thought to prepare me for what was to come. "The real Lucy Swinton died three days ago of typhoid fever."

I gasped.

"According to Mrs. Smith, who has, in her spare time, volunteered to nurse the sick and wounded at hospital wards around the city, Miss Swinton was utterly alone when she died. Her father was buried where he fell in Manassas. With any luck, Mrs. Greenhow would not know about her passing."

"With any luck," Mr. Pinkerton echoed.

I felt really, really sorry for the real Lucy Swinton, dying among strangers. And to know that her father had perished while she was so ill. My own father's face flew into my head. I was awash with such love for him and felt such a rush of relief that he was alive that it nearly took the breath out of me.

"How old was Lucy Swinton?" I asked.

"Only sixteen," Mr. Webster said softly.

A cold chill passed through me. A girl so close to my age! Of course, Mr. Webster took notice.

"Do not dwell on that sad event. Not now, or in the future, do you understand? You are to *be* her," he said.

"Yes, Mr. Webster." And I thought, *you are my fine tutor, my almost mind reader. Could you read my fortune in a gypsy globe as well? And would you tell me if you knew?*

"If Mrs. Greenhow accepts you," Mr. Webster went on, "she may well try to recruit you. She uses and discards young women like soiled handkerchiefs. If they vanish, she finds other zealous, angry souls who would die for the Confederate cause."

"And if she does try to recruit me?" I asked.

"Do not refuse," he said.

I felt a rustle of fear and excitement. These two quicksilver feelings were to become familiar. I learned to deal with them in time. They were like new friends dueling with my emotions.

"We will make every effort to protect you," Mr. Webster said.

"Have you got hold of all of this, Miss Lucy?" Mr. Pinkerton asked. I understood what he was doing and did not look startled when he called me by my new name.

"Oh, yes, sir." I dipped in a little curtsey I'd seen the girls on the street do as a gesture of respect. I'd never curtsied to anyone before, and it felt clumsy. I'd practice the silly movement, I promised myself.

Mr. Pinkerton rang a little bell that sat on the counter desk. At once, Mrs. Smith hurried in. She was holding a gleaming blonde wig in her hands.

"Undo your hair, please, Lucy," she said.

I did as she commanded. I have really long hair and curls that pop out like loose springs, remember? When I let it down, it tumbled over my shoulders and down my back.

She handed me pins with hooks at the end. "Pin it up."

I tried to roll my heavy tresses into a large chignon.

"No, hold your hair with your right hand. With your left, sweep it into a tight twist and secure the pins. Feel around it to make sure none of your own is peeking out. Don't remove the wig, even when sleeping."

I winced.

"You'll get used to it," she said, handing me a bright blue pork-pie cloth hat. "If you are in trouble, leave the hat upside down in the window of your room. If the drapes are drawn, leave enough room to display the hat. Greenhow will likely put you in the top floor nursery with her little daughter. If you change rooms, we will be watching the house from all sides."

Good, I thought with relief, there will be help if I need it. My relief was short lived.

"Only in a true emergency, Lucy, should you signal for help," Mr. Webster said. "We need to make this arrest as soon as possible, and make it stick. Mrs. Greenhow has many friends, many gentlemen of authority who would swear to her innocence."

"Yes, lass, even a Congressman enjoys her, um, favors. We believe she is worming Union secrets from him, the brazen hussy!" Mr. Pinkerton said, glowering.

"You will be messaged as *Dragonfly*, your code name within the organization. Do you understand? *Dragonfly. Wide-winged. Able to soar away.*

The wig was pinching my ear, and my mind was swarming with all I'd heard. Was I to be a sacrifice to the cause they so passionately believed in?

"May I see a looking glass, Mrs. Smith?" I asked, feeling around my head for stray hairs. They were all over the place.

"No. You have to be able to change in the dark, if need be."

111

Mr. Pinkerton handed me a carpetbag. "The rest of your attire is within. It is fine mourning garb. Of course, you will dress that way for as long as you are there, in memory of your departed father."

I shuddered. I wore black for Mama not that long ago.

"You'll manage the dress for yourself," Mrs. Smith interrupted my memory. "Before you leave here, secrete your weapon in the bottom of the bag, under the velvet material. The Greenhow woman might well have your person searched."

Before he left, Mr. Pinkerton quizzed me again, feeding me more facts about Lucy. When he was satisfied that I had retained all he wished me to know, finally, he said, "Be at the flower stand at daybreak. Watch Mr. Riley. He'll signal you. Two bouquets of violets mean the couriers have not been spotted. One bouquet? Leave immediately, return here, and wait for instructions. Are you ready?" Mr. Pinkerton asked.

"I am ready." I meant it. My nervousness was lifting. I imagined I saw myself—a lost little outsider with facts and names diving circles in her brain—the girl I used to be. She was applauding.

"Godspeed, Lucy," Mr. Webster said.

"Watch your back, Miss Swinton," Mrs. Smith added.

She led me to a small room. There was a cot, a blanket and a pillow. A piece of chicken and a bowl of soup sat on a table by the cot.

"Eat, rest here for a few hours, Lucy," she said. "You'll leave in the morning. Get used to lying down with the wig on."

She closed the door.

I looked at the black mourning dress, and the bonnet that looked like a rotted flower. Death, two deaths, actually, of two complete strangers made the air heavy with their presence; filled the room with shadows upon shadows. I ate what I could and tried to fall asleep. sleep. As I drifted off, I pictured myself in my new identity. Seventeen-year-old Lucy Swinton of Virginia. I said her name over and over.

Twenty

I awoke early, or rather Lucy Swinton awoke early, this Southern orphan, had a few last bites of leftover chicken. Then, holding a carpetbag of meager belongings, with my gun stored in a hidden compartment under a fold of leather and horsehair at the bottom, I straightened her dress and washed my face.

Before I left the empty photography studio, I paused for a moment at the door, adjusting her bonnet over the wig that had itched like the dickens during my sleep. I slumped a bit, my head bowed, as would have been Lucy Swinton's demeanor in this time of grief. Then I walked into the new morning.

When I neared the Greenhow house, I saw Mr. Riley watching from across the way, busily arranging his flowers. When he spotted me, he held up the same bunch of lilacs, twice. I remembered that meant Mrs. Greenhow's couriers were not about.

As I passed three Union soldiers standing guard at the foot of the stairs, I glanced at the front windows. The drapes were pulled shut, and no doll in petticoats sat in front of them. In case Mrs. Greenhow was watching me, I glared at one of the soldiers. He muttered something about a little Rebel and more. Well, let's just say that he called me a really vulgar name. The others chuckled.

I climbed the stairs to Mrs. Greenhow's door. I reached up and rang a large brass bell.

The door opened, and there Mrs. Rose Greenhow stood, straight-backed, tall and shimmering in teal-green velvet trimmed dress. She was full-figured, ivory-skinned and beautiful, with deep-set stony black eyes.

"I'm here to see Mrs. Greenhow, ma'am," I said, tingeing my voice with a bit of a southern accent. Of course, I'd recognized her, but I wasn't going to let on straightaway. She scrutinized me.

"And who might you be?" Her voice was low and musical. With her wide hoop skirt and narrow waist, she looked like a gilded bell.

"I'm Lucy Swinton, ma'am. I believe you were expecting me." I curtsied— at least I did what passed as one—and handed her the letter.

She stood in the entryway like a queen guarding a castle. When she finished reading, she put her hand out. "I am Rose Greenhow." Her smile was forced. But why shouldn't it be? Her house was guarded by Union soldiers and watched by Mr. Pinkerton's force. At any moment she could be arrested.

Did that make me feel for her? A little. From what I'd been told, she was zealously committed to the Confederate cause, almost like it had become a religion. I hoped these thoughts had not changed my demeanor, or make her see through me. I couldn't let my feelings show. But I had not lost my resolve. Not on my first mission. Not with what I'd been entrusted to do.

She took my hand. Was she ever going to ask me to come inside?

"I've not met Mr. Willard Duvall," she said, "though I surely knew his wife before she died of that dreadful lung affliction." She spoke quickly.

*She's testing me. Don't let her see I'm struggling to remember.*

"No, Mrs. Duvall passed of yellow fever, ma'am. It took her after only a few days."

I'd been told that by Mr. Pinkerton.

I waited.

Finally—

"Of course, she did. So many diseases, with no remedies, one becomes sadly confused." Mrs. Greenhow sighed. Her face relaxed. I was doing all right—so far. "Does Mr. Duvall have relations here in the city?" Her eyes held mine again.

*Think. If you don't know, say so. Breathe.*

"I'm sure I don't know, ma'am, but I am mighty grateful to him, hearing of my plight and all."

*Will one of the agents pull me out? Now?*

Mrs. Greenhow smiled. The breath I was holding whooshed out of me. I covered it with a cough.

"Of course, dear, we've been waiting for you. My 'little birds' told me so." She looked over my shoulder and sneered at the two soldiers who stood behind me.

For good measure, so did I. This time they didn't jeer or laugh. They clasped their rifles and looked daggers at us

Mrs. Greenhow whisked me into the entryway. At last, I was inside!

I noticed a young girl-child crouching behind a tall, wide-leafed fern. She was the spot-on image of her mother, right down to her tiny chignon and wide-hooped dress.

"Mama!" she cried. "Has she come to take you away?"

"It's all right, Little Rose," Mrs. Greenhow said. "This young lady is a friend."

I smiled at the child. She was whimpering. She must have been truly afraid.

"I'll take your cloak and bag, my dear," Mrs. Greenhow said before I could reach for the carpetbag. "Mourning clothes are a somber sight, and heavy," she said, running her hands over the cloak as if making sure it was not concealing anything. "We'll take your things to the room you'll share with my angel here."

"Mother!" the child cried out. "Don't open the door again!"

Mrs. Greenhow whispered to me, "Little Rose has become so fearful that they're going to take me to prison, or worse. 'Mama's hangmen,' she calls the dreadful people who skulk about our home day and night."

"How awful for you," I whispered back. And part of me meant it. No matter where her loyalties lay, she was a mother who loved her child. While I was getting sentimental about her, I ducked just in time to dodge a wooden whirligig toy Little Rose had thrown straight at my head.

I walked over and took the monster-tyke firmly by the hand. "Save that weapon for the Yankees," I said. "Oh, I call them dirty blue-bellied cowards myself." I was getting into my character all right.

Little Rose ran to the window, yanked it open and shouted my improvised slur straight at the soldiers.

Her mother smiled approvingly at me. With her arm firmly in mine, she led me into a front room filled with dark, shining wood cabinets and finely carved marble topped tables. A grand piano stood in the middle of the room. The child ran to it and began banging on the keys.

Mrs. Greenhow smiled. "You'll mind my little girl well, I pray, Miss Swinton. What with all the tensions of late, she is quite in a muddle, as you can see." The banging grew louder.

"Oh yes, I've been in a terrible muddle myself, ma'am," I said. "As you know, I lost my dear Papa at Manassas." I sniffled, hoping I looked properly sad. "I'm not sure if you knew that my mother has passed on as well."

"I did not," Mrs. Greenhow said. "Communication is . . . difficult these days."

That comment almost knocked me over. It seemed she was communicating, and then some. I kept talking.

"I've no way to move in the world now, orphaned as I am, ma'am, but I am well-versed in mathematics, and literature. I will surely teach your lovely child here many, many things."

"I'm not a child and I don't need a teacher!" Little Rose yelled, running over and pinching me on the leg. "I'll see to her, Mrs. Greenhow," I said, giving the little mite a sharp nudge with my foot.

The doll I'd noticed in the window a few days earlier sat by the door. "Oh, ma'am," I said, "this lovely doll here, why, I had one exactly like that, when I was just her age. Oh, I did love that doll so," I said, picking it up to see the many layers of colored petticoats.

"My mother made all my dolly's clothes," I said. "My dearest mother." Tears welled in my eyes, real tears for the first time that day, as my mama's face flashed in my mind, and the pain of losing her stuck in my heart like a burr.

"We're all a bit lost, then," Mrs. Greenhow said. "But not for long. Victory is at hand. Mark my words."

"I pray it will be so," I said fervently.

I did mark her words. Oh, I did indeed. And as we walked, I memorized the layout of her house. She led me up an ornate wooden staircase studded with fat, grinning cherub heads. She opened the door to a small room with two cots, two chairs, a blackboard and a small writing desk. There were tiny iron soldiers lined up facing each other on the floor. Some were lying on their sides.

"See how the Yanks have fallen at Manassas!" Little Rose said with glee. She knelt and grabbed up a miniature mounted horseman and pranced around the room. "Dead and gone!" she shrieked, "Dead and gone!" She tugged at my skirts.

"Wanna play? You be the dirty Yank and I'll plug you one." She thrust the soldier at me. "I stabbed you!"

Thankfully, her mother pulled the child to a chair. "None of that, Little Rose, Miss Swinton is here to be a companion, and, of course, she will help you with your lessons."

"Why do we have to sleep in my lesson room, mother?" Little Rose stamped her foot and yelled.

"So you won't have nightmares, darling. You don't mind do you, Miss Swinton? The bedrooms are downstairs and Little Rose swears she sees monsters outside the window. In fact, she probably does."

"Like this!" Little Rose made a hideous face. She grabbed the corners of her mouth and stretched the skin wide. Her eyes bulged out. Then, she screamed and dove under a cot.

"She'll come out eventually, I assure you, Miss Swinton." She gazed at her daughter wearily. "This is the only room without a true window, you see?"

Yes, I saw. There was only a small glass porthole window much too high for anyone to look through. And harder to signal from, I thought.

"I'll leave you two now. Oh, and if you need anything, ring this bell and I'll hear it downstairs. My serving woman has run off and left me." She whispered, "She claimed the soldiers peering at us day and night gave her a fright so bad that she fainted on the hour. I don't believe that. It was the abolitionists that spirited her away."

"I'm sorry, that must be hard for you," I said. I thought, *of course it is hard depending on servants to do your work, carry your slops buckets, and the like. Couldn't these types do anything for themselves?*

"Everything is a trial for me now," Mrs. Greenhow's shoulders dropped. All the brightness and poise was gone. "I don't know what will become of us." She left the room, closing the door behind her. "You will please remain with Little Rose, at all times, Miss Swinton?" she called from the hallway. "I can't have my child falling into their hands, now can I?"

"Yes, ma'am," I answered, locking eyes with Little Rose, who'd crawled out from under the cot and was about to empty her cup of milk on my shoe. "Don't even try," I told her after I was sure her mother had gone.

Little Rose backed away.

For a solid day, Mrs. Greenhow's daughter tormented me. She claimed not to know her multiplication tables, and repeatedly scratched at her desk with a hatpin. At least she didn't throw anything more at me.

The house cat, a gray tabby with a solemn, suffering gaze became a "Yankee soldier," and was repeatedly imprisoned in a linen trunk until it yowled for mercy.

But when Little Rose had fallen asleep after hiding a wad of sticky taffy in my boot, I looked carefully around the sparse room. I opened the trunk that had imprisoned the poor cat. It was completely bare except for a few balls of cat-fur. I remembered this was a sort of schoolroom, not a sleeping place.

My eyes lit on a high shelf. On it stood a candy jar stuffed with colored papers inside. On tiptoe, I was able to grasp it. I rummaged through the peppermint candies until I found a single white wrapper with no sweet inside. Something was scrawled on it in pencil. The outside of the wrapper was marked *copied and sent*.

I made out a circle with a dot in the middle. Under it, were these words: "St." and "Mc," followed by "BOW," and finally a sketch of a bull's head. I grabbed up a pencil, an unwrapped yellow piece of candy paper and copied the letters and the animal head on a piece of lined lesson paper on the child's desk. I quickly folded it and secreted it under my wig. I noticed that the candy wrappings were in only three colors: yellow, blue and red.

There was no sound from the hallway. Maybe her mother was still sleeping. I took a quick look out her bedroom window. There was so one about.

I nudged Little Rose. She rubbed her eyes sleepily and stuck out her tongue at me. I managed to wash her face and mine from a pitcher of water sitting on a dresser by the bed. I heard the sound of footsteps outside the door. It opened a crack and there stood Mrs. Greenhow. She looked as tired as I felt, with great circles under her eyes. She smiled weakly and handed me a tray with toast, milk, and two bowls of porridge on it. As she left, she closed the door. I realized she hadn't locked us in … yet.

I promised Little Rose a piece of candy if she would play a rhyming game with me, and I wouldn't make her recite her multiplication table anymore. It worked. The kid was a fiend for sweets.

I clapped my hands and whispered, "Yankee Doodle is a scamp, find him hiding in a camp. Come on, Little Rose, say it with me, okay?"

"Why do we have to whisper?"

"Because we're pretend soldiers, and we have a secret."

"Are we Yanks or Rebs?"

"Rebs, of course," I answered.

"Goody," she whispered. We recited my impromptu ditty again. "Another one, Miss Swinton!"

"Okay, here we go! I'll start. *To summon the lady strong and fair, what color should the dolly wear?*"

Little Rose eyed me suspiciously. Out came another piece of candy. "Blue," she said. "More candy."

"Nope, we're not done with the rhymes."

She pouted.

I was thinking fast now, making up rhymes on the spot. Oh, boy was I ever. "*And when she's red, what shall we say?* Come on Little Rose, you finish it!"

She grabbed the last piece of candy. "We tell the lady, go away!" she said, red peppermint bits all over her face.

"Wonderful! You are so creative! Isn't this fun?" I hugged the child. She hugged me back. That felt strange because I was beginning to like the little dickens.

First I had to be sure, and then I had to figure out how to get the color code to the agents. I had to be right. It was night. The child would soon be asleep. I looked again at the high window. There was a small latch attached to a long bar. The window opened out! I'd wait. The arrest wasn't coming until tomorrow. I pulled little Rose onto my lap. In case she rhymed before just to play the game and it didn't mean anything, I decided to probe further.

"My mama used to tell me ditties about two little Irish Leprechauns who had a secret. They were in charge of a pot of gold at the end of a rainbow. One of them wrote down all the colors of the rainbow, ending with one, so when he hid his pot of gold, only another leprechaun would know where to find it. In case something happened to one of them, of course."

I rocked her in my arms. It felt nice. I have to admit.

"Okay," she said sleepily, "I have one. But I can't tell anybody else."

"Of course not. I will never say anything."

She hesitated.

"I promise you, Little Rose."

"It's my special secret. Mama told me to keep the paper in case they took her away and left me. Will you take care of me if that happens, Miss Swinton?"

"Yes, I will. I promise." Her whole little body relaxed. She put her hand in mine. I hated to lie to the child, really hated it. "Tell me, sweetheart."

She spoke so softly I had to strain to hear her.

"*Green. Stay away. Blue. Take message. Yellow. Watch our door. Red. Danger,*" she said.

I hugged her. "Thank you for trusting me. We're friends now, right?"

"Yes," she said, nestling close to me. I stroked her hair and wrestled with my conscience over the lies I'd told her.

Now I knew that each color of the doll's petticoat was a signal. It was a perfect communication. Even I had to admire the sheer cheek of it.

When I was sure the child was fast asleep, I copied the color codes on a sheet of paper along with the odd letter patterns I'd written on the candy wrapping. I ripped a corner off my shawl, put a few of Little Rose's marbles into the ball I'd made, and climbed on a chair to reach the window. I opened it a crack. There was a soldier patrolling the back of the house. I threw out the ball. It hit the ground at his feet. He looked around, his rifle raised. I saw someone dressed in rags scurry over and take the balled-up material before he noticed.

Thank goodness. Now I knew Pinkerton's people, at least one of them, was there. I took a chance, then and tiptoed out the bedroom door to the parlor. The room was still, and sure enough, the doll was in the window. Its legs were splayed open with a petticoat showing clearly. It was blue, meaning a messenger was being summoned. A lit candle sat beside it. I stuffed the doll back in the window.

I heard her voice before she appeared. Mrs. Greenhow came in wearing a nightdress. She had a long hatpin in her hand.

"Is something wrong, Miss Swinton?" she asked, her eyes glowing like stoked embers. "And where is my daughter?"

"She's fallen asleep, ma'am," I said, gathering my thoughts. "I thought I heard someone at the door."

"Was someone at the door?" She neared me. Oh, did I have to think fast.

"Mrs. Greenhow, those soldiers out there. I hate them. Maybe one of them killed my father. If only I could find a way to get back at them!"

She studied me carefully, the lowered the hat pin and withdrew a tiny packet from her bodice.

"All right. Take this packet outside. If a soldier stops you, tell them you are ill and must go to the privy right away. Turn right at the first dogwood tree. They will not follow a young lady there. The privy is just by the tree. Go inside and put this under the seat. Come right back. I'll be waiting for you, Miss Swinton."

"Yes, ma'am," I said.

"Of course, if you don't return, I'll have to figure something happened to you."

"Yes, ma'am."

I took the packet and ran down the stairs, my hand clutching my stomach as though I was really ill. The soldiers were sitting on the ground smoking. As I ran by them, I made a gurgling sound, and for good measure and added a couple of groans.

"Don't puke on me now, miss," one said.

The other man laughed loudly.

I found the privy and put the packet under the seat. As I came out, someone grasped my arm. I pushed my attacker to the ground. When I bent down, to keep him or her still, in spite of the tattered clothing and torn straw hat, I saw it was Mrs. Warn.

"Go away!" I whispered.

"Are you all right?"

"Yes. Inside under the seat. There is a message for her courier. And the ball with the marble is her summoning code."

"I've got it. Greenhow sent you out here?"

"She sent me because I asked to go."

Mrs. Warn got up, rubbing her arm. Turn about is fair play, I thought as I remembered the bindings on my wrists. "Maybe we've got her this time," she said. "You've done well. Remember, we are all around you."

*Not if Mrs. Greenhow stabs me though the heart with a hatpin, you aren't*, I thought. I ran back to the house.

Mrs. Greenhow was pacing in the entryway.

"Were you stopped?"

"No. It went fine."

"Thank you, Miss Swinton. You are a true daughter of the South."

"God save them all, ma'am," I said.

She parted the curtain of the front window, and peeked out. I stood behind her with enough room to see as well. A tall, slender figure in a hooded cloak was walking quickly back toward the dogwood tree. Before she rounded the corner to the privy, two dark figures took hold of her. One wrapped his hand over her mouth. It was Betty! I recognized her walk, and saw the side of her face.

I turned to hurry away. Mrs. Greenhow grabbed me by the hair.

"It was a trap, wasn't it." Her grasp tightened. My head was forced back.

"You will pay for this. Above all others, you will pay," she said.

I felt the sharp point of the hairpin in my ear.

"If you resist, I'll pierce your brain," she hissed.

"I didn't have anything to do with it!"

"Shut up. Of course you did. No one knew when my courier was arriving. They were lying in wait for her. Because of you! Damn you!"

She forced me up the staircase. It was high and the way narrow. I had nowhere to go.

She was about to thrust me into a closet when Little Rose woke up.

"Don't be afraid, my darling," she said. "Miss Swinton," she snarled my fake name, "Miss Swinton and I are playing a little game. Come with me now. We're going away for a while!"

"I want to play the game!" yelled Little Rose, jumping into the closet with me just as her mother was about to lock me inside.

"No!" Mrs. Greenhow cried. "Come out, Little Rose, now!"

"I love games, Mama!" The child screeched.

I yanked her away from her mother and jumped into the closet with the child against me. "I'll hurt her if you come any further," I yelled. I slammed the door in Mrs. Greenhow's face and locked it.

"I don't like this game," Little Rose whimpered.

I heard loud voices then. Mrs. Greenhow screamed curses at whoever was there.

"It's all right!" a woman shouted. I didn't answer. How did I know who was really out there?

"Fiona!" I heard her call out.

Okay, that name did fine. I unlocked the door. Little Rose ran screaming into her mother's arms.

I saw a group of soldiers posted in the hallway, their rifles pointed into the room. And there was Mr. Pinkerton himself with Mrs. Warn and Mike.        I watched as a soldier dragged Little Rose and her mother, cursing, damning all Yankees, including me. And to make more of this raucous muddle, Mr. Pinkerton pushed a young disheveled woman in front of me. Her long blonde hair fell over her shoulders and tumbled down her back. She was sweating heavily, her face twisted, making sounds like a snarling animal. Even though her hands were bound, she raised both in the air. "God save the South, And may you all rot in hell," Betty Duvall hissed.

Twenty-One

"What made you come just then, sir?" I asked Mr. Pinkerton when I was taken to the photography studio soon after the capture of Betty and Mrs. Greenhow.

"When Betty took the packet, we grabbed her. Mrs. Warn kept a steady eye on your room—from a tree, I might add—well, she noted the blue petticoat in the window, and we waited for Betty. A doll, my God, a doll, right under our noses!" he exclaimed.

I do believe a wrinkling appeared at Mrs. Warn's lips. A smile? No, not yet.

He handed me the paper I'd copied from the child's room. "What do you make of this, Miss Bradford?" he asked. "Although this dispatch was already delivered by Betty to Colonel Jordan, this is not encoded. This is different."

I studied the pattern again. I blocked out everything else.

A circle with a dot in the center. Center, Center, Centreville. I remembered the woods behind the town Jake and I had encamped. Centreville. Yes.

Next: Mc. Mc, Mc. Who or what would that be? Who was at Centreville before the terrible Union defeat? Mc, Mc . . . McDowell, the Union General.

Next, the initial B, and the cow head sketch.

But was it a cow? No, it had horns. A Bull. Bull Run.

"The Confederate General Beauregard was to meet McDowell's troops at Bull Run!" I looked at the agents gathered around me.

"Is this how it happened?"

"Yes, the Rebels knew of the Union movement to Centreville, as did the newspapers, but because of Greenhow's courier, the Confederates were able to get word to Beauregard in time for him to reinforce with many more men."

"McDowell's men left Centreville with no idea they'd be met by a wall of Confederate soldiers who far outnumbered them," Mr. Pinkerton said, and added, "I must tell you, Miss Bradford, that Mrs. Warn came to the same conclusion. You are both to be commended." This time, Mrs. Warn shook my hand.

"Bravo, kid," Mike said, clapping me on the back.

"The Greenhow ring has been broken . . . for now," Mr. Pinkerton said. "But you, our exceptional young agent, will be in the gravest danger. Do you understand? We don't have Colonel Jordan. We don't have them all."

If I hadn't had Betty's sharp, loathing glower stuck like a nail in my brain, I'd have grown a foot at least, right in front of them. And if I hadn't wished to hold my father in my arms, or longed to rush to Jake Whitestone, wherever he was, and have Mama back, and transport Isaac and his frightened souls, and Nellie to a safe place, I'd have been able to feel true happiness.     There is no pure joy, Madeline Eve Bradford, I told myself. Was I right? Of course I was.

When I got back to my aunt's house, that's when I read about Jake.

*

**Special from the *New York Tribune*       Alarming News!  Our young scribe known to you as PAN has been captured by the Rebels!**

**Of his own volition and with the blessing of this newspaper, he'd secured an exclusive post with a band of Union scouts, an elite force that moves ahead of our troops, and relays critical information of the enemy's movements to their superiors.**

**Despite his companion's efforts to free him from Rebel hands, PAN was taken away. We are told that PAN resisted mightily, but to no avail.**

**Word has it that he has been transported to a Confederate Prison in Richmond.**

**These are alarming tidings. The prisons in the Confederate Capitol are in the keep of General John H. Winder, a most cruel and hard man, hated by his own people. This is dreadful news indeed.    Pray for PAN, for Mr. Greeley's great paper and all who represent it. We are considered the mortal enemies of the entire South.    Pray.**

The paper fell from my hands. I felt a whirling in my head. My mouth was dry, my heart thudded against my ribs. Jake in a prison! What would they do to him? Would he survive?

Then, I got really angry. Why did he put himself in such danger? Was he a fool? Or someone who needed the high excitement, needed the risk to feel like he was alive and a part of this terrible war—

Wait a minute, I told myself. Who are you thinking about? Jake Whitestone or yourself? Are you not risking every part of your being? Are you not in grave danger every time they send you on a mission? Every time!

Will any of us, my father, Jake and I, survive this? Was it worth it?"

"Is it worth it?" I shouted really loudly.

My aunt, who'd been dozing on the sofa, sat straight up, knocking a pile of needlework from her lap. It fell on the floor, along with her reading spectacles. "Oh, saints to goodness, Miss Madeline. You nearly stopped my heart with that scream." She fanned herself wildly with a pillow.

I just stood there breathing hard. I must have looked like a madwoman. "I'm sorry, Aunt Salome." I couldn't help it; a shrill voice came from my throat. "I'm really sorry!"

I headed straight for the cellar, down the stairs, and ran smack into Nellie. And Isaac. They were huddled together by the trap door. A large grain bag was on the floor between them. The top was open. I walked straight up to Isaac. He reached into his shirt, brandishing a knife. "No, Isaac!" Nellie said. "She's a friend to us." Nellie whispered, "Child, get away from him!"

"Is it worth it, Isaac?" I was close enough to see a crosshatch pattern of scars under his mouth. "Is it?"

He didn't raise the pistol he now held in his hand. "What do you think?" he said. He lifted his shirt to reveal a horseshoe-shaped mark that looked like a cattle brand. The scar was red and raised, like the devil himself had seared it there. Mr. Washington had a similar mark on his arm.

The grain bag heaved of its own accord. A woman's brown arm reached out. Isaac took her hand. "It's okay, Suzanne," he said gently, "we goin' now."

With that, he hefted the bag to his shoulders and pushed past me. Nellie opened the cellar door, and motioned to him. "Get gone, son. God go with you and the girl."

I sat down on the floor, exhausted, and sad, and proud of us all.

Yes, it was worth it.

Nellie moved about the kitchen, never speaking to me. Next thing I knew, she handed me a piece of cornbread with honey butter dripping down the sides. At that moment, it was the most delicious thing I'd ever tasted.

## Twenty-Two

The next day was a Sunday. Usually the bells of Mt. Olivet Church pealed loudly. Something was louder, drowning them out. Someone was screaming.

"An escaped lunatic! Lock the doors!" my aunt cried out as she peered through the window of the front parlor. A man was lying on the street, tearing away pieces of clothing with his teeth, growling and groaning, rolling in the mud. His head and face were bound with bloodstained bandages, nearly covering his nose. A bit of a gray-brown beard was barely visible. The man's cries were so loud they penetrated the heavy glass. As he thrashed, two policemen dragged him to his feet.

I opened the door a crack, hoping hard the man in the street wasn't Mr. Webster forced to quickly act this part to avoid detection. Because he posed in the Confederate capital as a trusted Rebel courier, I could only imagine what would happen to him here in Washington City if none of Pinkerton's men were alerted and could help him. There would be no way to tell what side he was on.    "If you are captured, Miss Madeline, you are on your own, as there is no certainty we can rescue you without exposure for us all," Webster had told me.    One of the soldiers kicked the man in the mouth. Blood spurted on the ground.    By now the man was squalling like a skinned rabbit. The bandage on his face had fallen off. It was not Mr. Webster, thank God. And he would not have screamed or squalled.    "No, for the love of God," the man cried, "I escaped from Saint Elizabeth's lunatic hospital! I swear it. Cock a doodle doooo!"    My aunt pressed against me at the door. It opened wider. She shouted to them. "Our cousin Herbert is in that asylum. He swears he's the King of Spain. Poor soul!"

"Shut it, ma'am," a soldier snapped. "This one ain't no king. He'll hang sure. He was nabbed just outside Georgetown sitting pretty on a Union officer's horse. The poor officer lay dead at his feet, see? Now close the door. Now!" I watched with a cold hand gripping my heart as the man was hog-tied face down, and dragged over the cobblestones. What if he'd been a spy? What if he had to kill the Union officer to protect a mission?

"Madeline! Help me pack up Mr. Whitestone's belongings. I'm placing a notice that his room is available," Aunt Salome ordered as she came toward me.

"Yes ma'am," I said. "It's not his fault he's not here." I had little patience for her now.    "What do you mean? He's gone derelict on me. What does he do, anyway?"    "He writes, Aunt Salome."    "Writes what?"    "For a newspaper. He's been captured by the other side." "And you know this because you saw it in a dream, Madeline?"    "I saw it in print, Aunt." "Of course you didn't, Madeline. Don't fib."    I was hardly able to control my anger. But if she knew I was devoted to the "Abolitionist Paper," as she called Mr. Greeley's *New York Tribune*,

126

I'd never hear the end of it.      "Yes, in a dream, Aunt." "Of course," she replied. "Nellie! Bring wood for the fireplaces. It is fall, in case you haven't noticed. "

I had, and a chill settled over me that no fire could warm.

## Twenty-Three

I woke to the sound of a gunshot, loud and close. Just after that, a wailing echoed throughout the house. I grabbed my revolver and ran toward the sound. When I reached the cellar, I saw Isaac lying on the floor, his head in Nellie's lap. Blood was everywhere, staining her apron and her hands. Before I could move toward her, a man lifted me off my feet, twisting my arms behind my back. My revolver dropped to the floor.     "No! No! My boy!" Nellie moaned.     "Shut up, Mammy!" a voice from the darkness called out.     "Frank! There's three over there." Another voice, ragged and harsh.     "Then get the ropes, fool. Truss them."     I struggled against the third man, but was no match. I bit his hand. Hard. He dropped me to the ground.     "Damn you! Whoeee, little tiger! Ain't you something." He aimed his boot at my head. On the ground now, I kicked back at him. He sat down on my legs, chuckling. "Whoeee."

The other two men tied up four Negroes: a man, two women, and last, a tiny boy-child. But the man, small and wiry, thrashed free of the rope and crawled to the door.     "Run, Hulbert!" the woman screamed.     As the man dove for Hulbert, he butted the slave catcher with his head. The man went down. They wrestled there as I groped for my gun. All the while, Nellie cradled her son. Isaac's head lolled, his mouth not moving.     The man stepped on my hand as I sat up and grasped the revolver. Sharp pains ran down my arm.     One threw open the kitchen door while the other slammed the butt of his gun into the slave's head. He lay still.     They retied him and dragged them all out into the alley. "Bounty on all three. Praise be!" the slave-catcher shouted. I got a good look at them then. One was fat and clean-shaven, with an anvil-shaped face; another was burly, with long whiskers and a red scar running over his cheekbone. The last was small and skinny with a hank of black hair that hung over his close-set eyes. I would not forget their faces. By then, Aunt Salome had rushed down the stairs.

Nellie was silent, rocking her son like an infant.     Aunt Salome went to her.

Nellie did not look up. She was shaking all over, tears streaming down her face.

Aunt Salome knelt next to Nellie and Isaac.

"Did you think I didn't know what was going on down here, Nellie?" Aunt Salome asked. "Of course I did. Though you may think I hate your race, slave catchers and their kind make me sick. I've seen too much cruelty, though my slaves were treated like family. And what's more, I didn't fear discovery. I don't give a tinker's damn what happens to me. I told no one. I swear on my life—not that it is worth much."

"It is, Missus Salome," Nellie said though her tears.

I could hardly believe my ears. My aunt knew about Isaac's activities!

I couldn't reason it then in all the chaos, but realized that nothing and no one are what they seem.

"He'll get a proper burial. I'll see to that," Aunt Salome said. "Anything broken, Madeline?"

I shook my head no. "Some cuts, that's all, Aunt." I was okay. It was Nellie who needed us now.          We wiped the blood from Isaac's face and then from the floor. We wrapped him in a blanket.

Finally, Nellie spoke. "I had got me the money enough to get my grandson. That's what I was fixing to tell Isaac. That's why I hung the quilt. I didn't know he'd come right back here. He wasn't supposed to. He changed it up. He changed it up."

I held out my arms to her. We wept together.

Twenty-Four

My aunt, Nellie and I buried Isaac in a colored cemetery, of course, as Negro folks couldn't even lie dead next to the whites of this city. How many times will I be dressed in mourning black? I shuddered.

We knelt before a headstone with Isaac's name etched on it, paid for by my aunt, a gift of sorts she could hardly afford. As we walked from the gravesite, I spotted a familiar figure over by a clump of trees.

"I'll catch up with you, Aunt Salome," I said, "I want to linger here for a moment." I pressed my aunt's hand to my lips. I had no words for what she had done and how I had misread her.

I watched the two women leave. My aunt's arm was around Nellie's shoulders.

When I was sure they'd gone, I hurried to Mr. Webster. I'd learned to spot my teacher from afar. He looked so tired, and much, much older. He moved stiffly—rheumatism, he said.

"Miss Madeline, Mr. Pinkerton wants you to know he was most saddened to hear about Nellie's brave son. Isaac's work will continue until all his people are free. Mr. Pinkerton promises that. That is the great task of this war."

"I know it is, sir."

Mr. Webster got up very slowly. His back was hunched. He grimaced in pain. "You are an able agent now, Miss Bradford. When I first met you, I saw a youngster of rare abilities. Now I see that you are becoming a strong woman."

"Thank you for being my teacher, sir. I could not have asked for better." I was flooded with emotion and pride. "Are you going back to Richmond?"

"Oh, yes," he said, sighing.

"I'll go with you!"

"You cannot. Mr. Pinkerton is sending Jane Smith with me. We will be posing as husband and wife. I've prepared my Confederate contacts there for the arrival of my "wife." I've gotten her a job as a clerk in their war department. It is a complete infiltration, as Mr. Pinkerton would say."

Was I envious? Oh, yes, but after all, I was a newcomer. Mr. Webster and Jane Smith were part of the early force, Mr. Pinkerton's best, and all seemed arranged.

I must have looked downcast. "There is much for you to do here, Miss Madeline. But be on alert at all times." He touched my face.

"Do you know anything about Jake Whitestone, Mr. Webster?"

"When he wrote in his last dispatch that Richmond was 'The Kingdom of the Cruel,' the Confederates I have cultivated there vowed he would be captured and imprisoned. I could not stop them."

"Is he still there?

"I don't know. I hope not. A Richmond prison is a terrible place to be. I'll do what I can to help Mr. Whitestone. Goodbye, Miss Madeline."

He said goodbye with such finality, it was like a ghost had floated out from a grave and passed right though him.

A low billow of fog drifted over the grass. He walked away into that fog.

*

*Remember when I told you about my nightmare? Here is how it really happened.*

I stayed in the cemetery until it was nearly dark, just sitting on the ground and thinking about all that had happened to me. I was so lost in thought that I did not sense her approaching. That was a grave error. I vowed I would never let it happen again.

"Turn around," a female voice whispered. "Now." Before I could duck away, or kick back, or grab her arm, I felt a gun against my head.

I turned slowly, my hands in the air.

*I faced her full on. I gasped. We are so alike: Wide set blue eyes, rambling brown curls, and tall, close in age —young, we are young. We are wearing wrinkled black frocks that hang loose on our thin frames. Are we in mourning, or in disguise? We might pass for sisters. But I don't have a sister, not a living one.*

I locked eyes with her, planning my next move. She cocked her pistol.

I ducked down, and darted past her. She fired at me. The bullet grazed my hair. I heard her panting hard behind me like a slave-tracking hound after its quarry. I turned and slammed my boot into her knee. She fell; her weapon flew out of her hand, and into the grass. I grabbed it. I put my foot on her back. She thrashed, cursing.

I yanked her up by the arm, my gun in her side. "Walk," I ordered. She stamped down hard on my foot. "No! Damn you, Yankee devil,"

"You'll never see tomorrow," the girl whispered as we fought. I reached for her head, but my hand slipped to the ruffling at the top of her bodice. It ripped apart. A piece of rolled up paper fell from the tear and dropped to the ground. I grabbed it up and jammed it down into my boot.

She kicked me hard in the side, knocking me to the ground. Then she leapt up and ran. I crawled after her, breathing hard. Just as I reached her, she yanked up a wooden door that was on the ground and pushed me into a big hole.

The skirt of my dress caught on splintering wood as I plunged into inky darkness, grasping for anything to break my fall. Something hit my face, something long. It was a rope with a bucket attached to it. I was falling into a well! I

133

could hear water bubbling and sloshing below me. I grabbed the rope and held on with all my strength.

"Night, night, little darlin'," she called out, her laughter echoing in the well until she slammed the wooden door shut. I heard the heavy thuds of rocks being piled above, sealing me in. And then, there was dead silence. Any jot of sympathy for this rebel left me. *You are not going to die here,* I told myself.

I took long, deep breaths to quiet my tumbling mind. I imagined my hands were made of iron and my legs were like twisty snakes. So like a monkey on the trunk of a thin palm tree I pulled and grasped and heaved and hoisted myself up the rope. I twisted my body, until I was upside down. When my feet touched the trapdoor, I kicked at it. Hard.

The door flew open an inch, but the weight of the rocks on top slammed it shut again. Still holding fast to the rope, I swung my legs until finally, on the last heave, the rocks flew off the trap door. I pulled myself over the edge and landed in a soggy pile of pine needles. My eyes were fixed on the darkness, my ears strained for slightest sound.

I crouched down, testing my legs and moving my aching arms, the torn skirt of my dress dragging on the ground; my mess of curls dripping with leaves.

As I was crawling along, I spotted the Rebel girl clawing at the grass, searching for her lost dispatch. Before she could move, I pinned her, face down, my body lying across hers. She bucked and scratched as I held her down. Straddling her, with one hand I ripped a piece of cloth from my skirt and bound her hands behind her.

I pulled her to her feet. "Welcome to the Union, little darlin'," I whispered in her ear. She kicked me hard in the shin. I pushed her along. My bosses' headquarters wasn't far. Out of the darkness, a hard little hand gripped mine. I went to bite down on whomever it belonged to when—

"Ouch! Cut it out! It's me," he said. "We've been looking all-the-heck over for you." The little hand with a bite mark on it was attached to a small, well-muscled arm that was attached to a tiny body topped by a jaunty, round face under a battered slouch hat.

No wonder I didn't sense Mike close to me. His stealth was legendary by now.

"We have to get her dispatch to headquarters," I said, holding out the tiny rolled up paper. The girl cursed again.

I pulled some kind of a wiggly black bug from my curls. It skittered away.

"What's your name, Miss Reb?" Mike asked. The girl was mute, head down, eyes shut.

"She ain't talking yet, but she will, kid." He grinned.

134

"When are you going to stop calling me kid?" I was careful not to say his name, at least not in public in front of a rebel agent.

Sure Mike's best cover is as a little boy, but really! Kid? Did he forget I'm almost sixteen, or what?

"Sheesh, touchy, ain't you?" Mike said, pulling another two bugs from my hair.

"Maybe these insects are Rebs. Can't be too sure, right?" He nudged the girl and squashed a bug under his tiny boot. She winced. Her fancy bonnet hung in tatters. Her dress was just as messed up.

"Did you have to kill them? I asked.

"The Rebs or the bugs?" Mike's voice hardened. He squashed the other one.

"What do you think?" He said to me. "You got lucky this time. You're alive, right?"

"This time, Mike." I said. This time. And that's why I'm writing this all down. In case there isn't a next time.

*

Mike and I pulled the girl along until I reached the photography studio. Mr. Pinkerton said someone on the force would always be there if help was needed. Sure enough, Mr. Riley came out of the darkness. Even if he had not, I knew I could have handled her.

Inside, the girl collapsed in a chair, her head down. "This time," I said to her, "this time we win."

Mr. Riley pulled the girl up by the arm.

"What is your name, girl?" he asked.

She fell forward, her foot unable to support her weight.

She was mute.

"The interrogators will get plenty more," Mr. Riley said, lifting her into his arms and carrying her toward the door. "Damn you," she said, spitting words like bullets at me.

Her face was ashen, but defiant. The door slammed behind them.

Mr. Pinkerton came into the room. I was decoding her dispatch. He was looking over my shoulder. Black letters of the alphabet tracked across the page. Both sides sent these swift secret jottings: A pattern of single letters of the alphabet, out of order, arranged in a square, like the shape of an animal pen. If you look at the first letters, and track down to the next, you can figure out what letters correspond to the first line on the square. Keep going, up and down, until they make a pattern, and reveal a key word that unlocks the code.

*This is what it said. :*

**Yanks on to Richmond. 10,000 man force. Meet with 20,000 of ours at the Rappahannock.**

135

"Maybe the Rebels will not be warned. Maybe we'll take the enemy city," Mr. Pinkerton said. "Good, Lass, good."

He handed me a hot cup of tea. A strong brew, tinged, I swear with a bit of whiskey. It warmed me to my bones.

"You'll need a new location for a time," He said. "They'll be back for you with others unless we find the rest of them first."

"Yes, sir," I answered, wiping the girl's face from my mind. I must have looked troubled. You couldn't look troubled in front of Mr. Pinkerton.

"Do not weaken, Madeline," he said. "For every one of us, there are at least the same number of them willing to die for their cause."

"You'll go back to the boarding house under guard. Pack your things."

Did President Abraham Lincoln's chief of detectives look tender and almost fatherly at that moment? Perhaps. But don't be fooled, as you know, he is a hard man, and a master deceiver. We all are now.

Twenty-Five

While Mr. Pinkerton's guard waited outside the boardinghouse, I packed my things. Where would I be sent, and for how long?

The house was still. Aunt Salome had gone to stay with her sister.

"Where will you go, Madeline?" she'd asked before she left.

"Mr. Webster has arranged lodgings for me. I'll be fine." I promised that if she didn't come back to the boardinghouse, when the war was over, I would visit her. I meant it.

"I will never forget what you did for Nellie and her son, Aunt Salome. Never." I hugged her goodbye. She was trembling. I could feel her bones, her thinness under my hands. She looked so very old to me.

Now, as I was closing my trunk, I heard footsteps. I held my weapon and followed the sounds. Had someone had gotten past the guard?

His back was to me.

"Stop," I said, holding my gun on him.

He turned around.

"Don't shoot!" Jake Whitestone said, raising his hands.

I lowered the gun. I wanted to rush into his arms. I couldn't rush into his arms. I had to go.

I thought, *don't love a spy. Don't love me.*

"You are free, Jake," I said instead. "Thank goodness."

"Maybe not goodness. Try someone important pulling some strings. I don't know who."

"Did they hurt you?"

"Not like things I saw them do to others." He shuddered. "I promised the Rebels that when I got back to Washington City, I'd try to be more objective in my reporting."

"Will you?"

"I don't know. The people of Richmond are not to blame. Their leaders are."

I wanted to hold him. I couldn't hold him. I looked away. I had to go.

"Keep looking at me, Madeline," he said. "Then I'll know that you are real."

I turned to leave. He pulled me to him. "Hellcat," he whispered.

He kissed me, then: My first one, ever. My lips, my whole body was on fire.

"I have to go now, Jake."

He didn't stop me. "Whatever you are doing, Madeline, when you are through, we will find each other.

"Yes." And I knew we would, if we survived.

\*

I walked out of the boardinghouse. Mike was waiting for me on the stairs.

"What took you so long, kid? I think I grew an inch waiting."

"Knock the kid stuff off, once and for all, Mike, okay?"

"Sure, sure. My mistake. Yeah. A kid you're not, now that I get a good gander at you."

There was a carriage waiting across the street. I handed the driver my bag. As the door opened a cloud of cigar smoke floated into my face. I settled into the seat. Mike was on one side Mr. Pinkerton, on the other.

"Perhaps Mr. Whitestone might be persuaded to join us one day," he said. "What do you think, lass?"

Madeline Eve Bradford was overjoyed at the thought. Maybe a little nervous, but mostly, overjoyed. The spy known as *Dragonfly* said she'd have to think about it.

**Special From the *New York Tribune***

**Dear Readers,**

**In case you were fretting over my disappearance and capture, your humble reporter is free.**

**Freedom. I am guilty over my freedom. Bear with me.**

**I was housed in an old tobacco warehouse that was converted to a prison. The place was dank and sorrowful. Union soldiers who were swooped up by Rebels after the defeat at Bull Run, deserters from the Confederate army and those sorry men and women who have displeased General Winder's detective thugs are all still festering there.**

**Why was I released? I don't know. Perhaps some influential sort from deep within the Richmond government had a hand in it. If I ever know his identity, I will thank him from the bottom of my heart. After the war, that is, when I pray we will be one country again.**

**For now, at the behest of my employer Horace Greeley, I have agreed to take a bit of a rest. "To gather your wits," he said. "And decide if being a flat out Union supporter is worth the risk."**

**Well, my wits are gathered. I'm young and strong. It is worth the risk.**
**PAN**

## Twenty-Six

I'm in a secret location. I'm sorry I can't even tell you where it is. Two of Mr. Pinkerton's guards are patrolling outside the hideout. Don't worry; my father thinks I'm safe. When Aunt Salome closed up the boardinghouse, Mr. Pinkerton's friend wrote a lovely letter inviting me to board with her and tutor her child. We sent word to my father about what had occurred at the boardinghouse. When he came on his soldier's day pass, a woman in spectacles, a small woman with a diligent, serious manner greeted him. It was one of Mrs. Warn's best disguises, I thought. She promised him I'd be well cared for, and paid for my work.

I was itching to leave, but knew I could not. I was gazing at the fire, wondering what book to read next. I'd just finished Miss Bronte's Jayne Eyre and was picturing Jake Whitestone as a young Mr. Rochester, all dark and dour, when the door opened and Mr. Pinkerton walked in and came straight up to me. His face was grim.

"First, Miss Bradford, you are to remain here for now. Mr. Washington will replace Mike." He motioned to a tall, middle-aged Negro man with an anvil-shaped jaw and a hard set to his eyes.

"I'm to keep a watch on you, Miss," Oliver Washington said.

I was trapped and knew there wasn't a darn thing I could do about it.

Mr. Pinkerton pulled a chair up close to me.

"Listen well, lass. The rebel girl you captured has sworn to find you, to kill you.

*Of course she has.*

"Did you learn her name, sir?"

"We will. She is a hard one."

"Was she harmed during the interrogation?"

"We do what we have to. Do not ask such a question again."

"Yes, sir."

If I were captured … I tried not to dwell on it. Mr. Pinkerton must have read my mind.

"Do not think about what the enemy might do to any one of us. It serves no purpose."

"Yes, sir."

"The girl was sent up from Richmond. We know this much: After a drunken Union soldier assaulted her, she killed him—effortlessly. He has been punished. Deservedly so. She was observed and recruited. Her training began."

*I might have done the same.*

No one has ever captured her. Until you."

*I know.*

"I have noted that you closely resemble one another. Odd, that. There the likeness ends, surely, eh?"

*I don't know where it ends.*

"They promise girls like her that for every Yankee agent they capture or assassinate, they will be rewarded personally and their families will be taken care of should they not survive. That is all we know so far. I don't doubt there is more."

"What about Betty Duvall and Rose Greenhow?" I asked, and wondered, how many more there were.

"They remain incarcerated. Mrs. Greenhow's daughter is very ill. That preoccupies her sufficiently."

I felt a stab of pity for the nasty little mite.

"And we have determined Betty is not nearly as lethal as the girl in our custody. Betty has begged our forgiveness, and has taken the oath of allegiance to the United States. A noble gesture, but in prison she stays."

Finally Mr. Pinkerton lit a cigar. With all the talk of prison and killing, the smell of the smoke was familiar and strangely comforting. But the look on his face was not comforting at all.

"There is a large bounty on your head, Miss Bradford."

Mr. Pinkerton rose. "There is something else. I have not heard from Mr. Webster or Mrs. Smith since they went to Richmond. That is very unusual"

Mr. Pinkerton was mighty worried, but he tried not to show it. Mr. Webster always told me that one day any of us might not come back. That offered me no comfort at that moment.

I vowed then and there to find a way to get to Richmond to find out what had become of him.

"Oh, Miss Bradford, Mr. Pinkerton said, with a half-smile, which for him was like a full one. "I nearly forgot, there is someone here to see you."

"Me?"

I couldn't believe my eyes. Jake Whitestone came into the room! He looked like the devil, unshaven exhausted and—Mike was right behind him, flashing a thumbs-up sign to me. Mike told me they "captured" Jake, and he tested really fine! Jake looked elated, and a bit shaky. I know the feeling.

"I suspected you had another life going, Miss Madeline." Jake said.

"Are you going to work with us?" I couldn't believe what I was asking.

"Looks that way. I can still do my reporting, but Mr. Pinkerton says I will be of great value. It's truly my war now, Madeline, just like it is yours."

I know just what he meant.

Mr. Pinkerton patted Jake on the shoulder, turned on his heel and left trailing cigar smoke behind him.

\*

Mike was cleaning a rifle, humming Dixie.

"Catchy little tune, isn't it? When we win this war, I hope we capture the song along with all the soldiers they have left." He set the rifle down and picked up a long, sharp, hunting knife.

"Can't be too well armed." He said.

Mr. Oliver Washington was standing by the cabin door. He looked uneasy, and never smiled.

Jake Whitestone settled next to me on the sofa.

"Don't worry about anything. I'll take care of you, Madeline." He said, groggily. Before I could reply, or argue, he was fast asleep.

"I'll take care of myself," I whispered, brushing back a wisp of a black curl that had fallen over his brow.

I guess I can tell you that the sun was setting over a bluebell-studded meadow. Through the window, I saw the guards walking back and forth.

It would be really quiet, peaceful, even, if Mike would stop humming.

Will she slip past them, glowing like fox fire through the trees on her way to find me, to do battle with me? It is not over between us, that I know.

*I fear it will be a long war, Miss Bradford, Mr. Webster told me once. Should you survive, you will have many more missions. You must continue to muster up all that you are, and all that you know to keep fighting this righteous battle.*

I *will* keep fighting. Whatever happens next, I am ready

OPTIONAL PIECES TO ADD HERE AS DESIRED…

A NOTE FROM JANE SINGER TO READERS

Her timing was perfect. She gazed at me from a 19th Century hand-tinted ambro-type,— cool-eyed, aloof and solemn with a tiny mark on her forehead in the shape of a comet or a falling star–a teenage girl lost in time. She'd been resting for who knows how long in a dusty case in the back of a used bookshop. I like to think she was waiting for me.

I'm a tale spinner - a novelist and a researcher. I'm hooked on all things Civil War, and have been ever since I was a little kid prowling around battlefields, never wanting to leave, and somehow knowing that the war that began one hundred and fifty years ago would always be important to me.

 I'm especially interested in the spies who worked undercover, different kinds of soldiers who provided intelligence and helped the effort for both the Union and Confederate sides. So when I found the photo, I was in the middle of outlining a book about a fifteen-year old spy I called Madeline Eve Bradford, a lonely, home-bound misfit with an amazing memory. Maddie landed smack in the middle of Civil War DC and found her true calling as a Union agent working for Detective Allan Pinkerton.

Even better, I learned that Pinkerton was the first in US history to hire women, not just as clerks, but as detectives. He used his teenage son as a dispatch carrier and had several women of unknown ages working for him when he started his detective agency in Chicago, even before he became the top spy in DC, so I took the liberty of having him hire Maddie. And I gave her a voice.

Writing in the first person is my favorite way to tell a story. As an actor, when I play a role, I think a lot about the characters. Not just what they look like, but how they sound, the way they move, what gives them the shivers, how they love, or shine, and what choices they make.

While Maddie, Jake, Nellie, Mike, Aunt Salome, Isaac and Summoner Bradford — some of the other people you've met in Alias Dragonfly— are fictional characters, they are based on stories of some of the spies Pinkerton used. But in Alias Dragon-fly, they do not change the course of history. Nope. Don't want to do that. Instead my bunch move though real events in real time, in a very real world; interacting with people who actually existed during the Civil War.

I'll list the real players here so if you want to know more about them, have a look at the list of books I recommend.

### Who Was Really Who

(Researching the lives of spies can be really challenging. They obscured their identities, created blinds appeared and disappeared like wisps of smoke.)

Allan Pinkerton: Chicago detective, and the head of General George McClellan's secret service. (You can read all about "Little Mac.")

Timothy Webster: Maddie's trainer, Detective Pinkerton's top spy. His story is big, scary, and ultimately very sad. You'll learn more about Timothy in the next book in the series, Alias Sparrow Hawk.

Kate Warn: The head of Pinkerton's female detectives. I've done a whole lot of work on the mystery of Kate. Check out my website for more details of how I uncovered her true identity.

"Hattie Lawton," was probably an alias. I think she was based on a very fearless young spy in Pinkerton's autobiographical account of his time in the war.

Mrs. Smith and Agnes Crawford: I found these women in an 1860 DC census living with Kate Warn. A biography of Pinkerton said Kate ran a training center for spies at the beginning of the war.

Rose Greenhow, and "Little Rose." Mama Rose was a society matron in DC. She was able to worm secrets out of the politicians and Union officers she hung around with, and pass intelligence straight through enemy lines to the Confederates. She was a big deal. "Little Rose' was, well, a passionate kid who hated Yankees for what they did to her mom. Can you blame her?
Rose writes that she had a female Pinkerton detective in her house before she was taken to the Old Capitol Prison. So, I got Maddie inside. Her saga continues. Like the young men and women working behind the lines in our tested by war and loss, she will be forever altered, as will I.

Jane Singer

# READING LIST

The Civil War is such a popular subject. Thousands of books, and counting have been written about it so picking some can be overwhelming. My own home library is crammed with just about every aspect of the war you can imagine and I haven't even scratched the surface. So where to start? Here are some books that will give you the basics and then some. It's how I started. Most are in libraries and some are ebooks now. How good is that?

## The Basics

Davis, Kenneth C. *Don't know Much About the Civil War.* Perennial: An Imprint of Harper Collins Publishers: 2004.

Gaffney, Dennis and Gaffney, Peter. *The Civil War.* Hyperion: New York: 2011.

Ward, Geoffrey C. *The Civil War: An Illustrated History.* Based on a documentary film script by Geoffrey C. Ward, Ric Burns, and Ken Burns. Alfred A. Knopf: New York, 1889. (A beautiful big book. If you want to see it come to life, watch Ken Burns film series, "The Civil War.")

## About Spies

Winkler, H. Donald. Stealing *Secrets: How a Few Daring Women Deceived Generals, Impacted Battles, and Altered The Course of the Civil War.* Cumberland House, 2010.

Markle, Donald E. *Spies and Spymasters of the Civil War.* Hippocrene Books, New York: 2000.

Mackay, James. *Allan Pinkerton:The Eye Who Never Slept.* Mainstream Publishing: Edinburg and London: 1996.

Van Doren Stern, Philip. *Secret Missions of the Civil War.* Bonanza Books: New York: 1959.

Blackman, Ann. *Wild Rose: Rose O'Neale Greenhow, Civil War Spy.* Random House Publishing Group. New York: 2005.

Varon, Eliazbeth R. *Southern Lady, Yankee Spy.* Oxford University Press, 2003.

Kline, Michael J. *The Baltimore Plot: The First Conspiracy to Assassinate Abraham Lincoln.* Westholme Publishing, 2008.

Blanton, DeeAnne *They Fought Like Demons: Women Soldiers in the American Civil War.* Louisiana State University Press: 2002.

Pinkerton, Allan. *The Spy of the Rebellion.* G.W. Carleton & Company: New York, 1883. (A word of warning: Pinkerton wrote this book long after the war ended. He loved a good story and because many of his papers were destroyed in the Chicago fire of 1971, the rest are in the Library of Congress, you should take him with a grain of salt.)

## ACKNOWLEDGEMENTS

To my wonderful family, for their love, their support, for putting up with my endless hours spent on "that old war." Chuck Eckstein, Jessica Masser, Lisa, Miles and Raleigh Singer, Hariet Eckstein, Missy and David Burgess, and Judy Oppenheimer.

My cherished friends: Larry Masser, John Stewart, Mike Nelson and Susan Chieco, Susanne and Marty Malles, Simone Study and Clay Holmes, Heth, Jed and Rhoda Weinstein, Erik Seastrand, Joanna Rubiner, Becky Bonar, Ken Deifik, Candace Michaels, Sharon Vincuilla and all the angels of Lend A Paw and New leash On Life, and Dr. Sandra Fallon.

And my fellow "history detectives," John Stewart, David W. Gaddy, Laurie Verge, John Stanton, Joan Chaconas, and Professor Robert S. Davis.

To my agent Robert Astle, Deborah Smith and Debra Dixon of Bell Bridge Books, Dee Dee De Bartlo, Gretchen Crary, Corinne Ray of February Partners, and Joel B. Michaels. Thanks and more to all of you.

And of course to Caspy, our brave and whimsical social therapy dog, and Angus, the sweetest four-legged creature I've ever known.

Made in the USA
Charleston, SC
19 October 2011